MURDER
SWINGS
THE
TIDE

MURDER SWINGS THE TIDE

LINDA SHIRLEY ROBERTSON

Coastal Villages Press
Beaufort, South Carolina

Tabby Manse ™

Published by Coastal Villages Press,
a division of Coastal Villages, Inc.,
PO Box 6300, Beaufort, SC 29903,
843-524-0075, fax 843-525-0000,
a publisher of books since 1992.
Visit our web site: www.coastal-villages.com.

Available at special discounts for bulk purchases
and sales promotions from the publisher
and your local bookseller.

Cover designed by Barbara Martin

ISBN 1-882943-20-1
Library of Congress Card Number: 2003112225

First Edition
Printed in the United States of America

and

*For Mr. Henry,
my Southern gentleman*

Clairene Aiken

"Swing With The Tide"

Linda Shirley Robertson

Acknowledgments

I would like to thank friends and family from Greenville, South Carolina, without whose guidance and faith I would never have finished this book. A special thanks to Eleanor, who wrote the note, "Keep on keeping on." My writing group with Brenda and Sue and Wednesday afternoon was inspirational for me. Sandy, Pam, and Sydney gave me support during my writer's blocks. A grateful nod to my editor, Barbara Martin. She kept the alligators out of my path. I am indebted to the gym and all my workout buddies who made me want to show up and get writing energy for the day.

Linda Shirley Robertson

Murder Swings the Tide

One

From her lounge chair on the beach house deck, Maggie Stewart relaxed and stretched her long, tanned legs. The afternoon sun beat fiercely on the exposed parts of her body. She could hear the steady rhythm of the ocean waves, but her mind continued in the work mode. It would take several days of vacation to calm the stress that churned inside her. Thoughts marched across her brain like advertising bullets on a brochure. Arden Interiors. Resign or stay in a stale situation? She knew she needed to forgive her ex-fiancé, though he had broken her heart, and get on with her life. But what life? The only life she had now was work, and working for clients who were more worried about status than style was less and less satisfying.

She hadn't dated for almost a year, not since she had found Brian in bed with her best friend, Mandy. She had little desire to date or even to socialize. How could she bother to make small talk with people or try to get to know anyone new when she was achingly aware now that people were capable of such betrayal? A year ago, Maggie had thought her life was nearly perfect, and now she wondered if there was anything in it that really mattered.

A large wave from the incoming tide crashed onto the beach. The sound jarred Maggie back into her present reality. Maybe Grandmother Harcourt was right. Men, you can't live with them and you can't live without them. At least her ex and his new bride wouldn't be living in Rosemont. If she changed jobs, she wouldn't either. She had this wonderful house and a few weeks to relax and sort through her decisions. Her dear friends Greg and Marilyn Meyers had loaned her their beach house. She had plenty of time to make rational decisions.

Maggie turned over onto her back and noted the strap marks from the chair on the lower part of her legs. She wiped away the sweat that was streaming into her eyes. The radio announced the time and reported the sweltering temperature with a chance of a late afternoon shower. Time to take a jog before the rain came. She had arrived a few hours ago and had seen a small portion of the lush, five-mile island.

Modern-day Seaward Island, South Carolina, began as a development for the enrichment of a few mainland families. The recession hit and progress halted. It was still an isolated island paradise. According to Marilyn, a tennis club, the Seward Inn, a local saloon, and the Kash and Karry Grocery were the extent of the island's entertainment. State funding for a bridge from the mainland had not materialized. People who lived in the small community commuted by ferry to the mainland.

Glorious silence, interrupted only by the crashing waves, was all that Maggie could hear. Arden Interiors was miles and miles away. Maggie's stress melted into the sweat on the lounger. She was a trifle annoyed when the sudden sound of a phone ringing in the kitchen pierced the stillness. The portable was on the kitchen counter. Pushing the sliding glass door open, she jumped over the counter bar stool, shoved the door shut, and padded across the cold tile of the kitchen floor.

The onslaught of frigid air popped goose bumps over her bikini-clad body. She grabbed the phone and tried to reach for her beach cover-up. "Hello."

"Ms. Stewart? This is S.J. Styles," a sultry female voice announced. It was a husky, Lauren Bacall-type of voice, the kind that betrayed years of cigarette smoking. "I live beside you in the pink palace. At least that's what my art protégés call it. Marilyn told me to be on the lookout for you. If you need anything let me know."

"Thank you. You must be Sondra Jean, the artist. I'm looking forward to my vacation on Seaward." Maggie balanced the phone on her knee and stuck her head through a terry pullover.

"Tomorrow night at six o'clock," she heard S.J. saying as she put the phone back against her ear. "I'm having island friends over. We'd all love to meet you. There aren't many of us, you know. Of course, we never include the locals. They're, well, a rowdy bunch. While you're here, I'd like for you to give me some ideas for my study. I don't want it to look like the Library of Congress. It's so difficult to decorate a study in a beach setting, don't you think? We'll discuss it tomorrow night, casual, of course. See you then. Ta ta." The line went dead.

Maggie stared at the phone for a few seconds. She felt stress creeping back into her shoulders and neck. What had Marilyn told the community? Makeovers by Maggie were available for all? Redecorating island houses was not on her agenda. For that matter, she didn't even give free advice to her friends.

She knew she'd have to go to the party if she planned to vacation here. She'd get Marilyn for this one.

Maggie flounced out of the beach jacket. She paused for a minute to admire the sky over the ocean through the sliding glass doors. Streaks of pink mingled with fluffy, white clouds.

After tying the laces of her running shoes and stretching her legs, Maggie jogged down the main road toward the Seaward security gate. The house key bumped against her thigh. Tomorrow she'd fasten it to her shorts with a safety pin. For the moment, it felt secure in her pocket. She looked up and realized the gate was in front of her.

"Afternoon," the guard called out. "If you be planning to run through them marshes over yonder, I'm advised to tell you not to. Them 'gators are mighty hungry and like fresh, young meat." His leering chuckle filled the air.

15

Maggie gave him her famous "I'll hang you like a drapery if you mess with me" look. Very effective for clients who wanted to change the color of the walls after they'd been painted. It had no effect at all on the guard.

Ignoring his lustful leer, Maggie headed down the narrow jogging path that cut through the marshes. A landscape architect wouldn't put a trail near unsafe swamps, she thought. The security guard had probably used that line on a lot of unsuspecting women.

The entire area seemed to be environmentally secure. No alligators on the trails. Green stop signs blended with the natural foliage. Spanish moss gathered around cypress branches. Palmetto trees sprang from the ground along the narrow trail. The swamp was quiet.

Gaining momentum, Maggie jogged around the bend, the guard forgotten. The euphoric jogger's high swept over her. Late afternoon disappeared, and she instinctively knew that she had reached the island's interior. The island from this point to the ocean was pristine, unspoiled by unnecessary human pollution. Salty air teased her nostrils. Marsh grasses waved. A blue heron called to its mate.

The seasonal spring tide sent a backlash of brackish water into the maze of lagoons that ran along either side of the jogging trail.

Along the right bank of the marsh lagoon, Maggie saw a flash of red ribbon. It translated in her brain as the perfect color for Jean Monroe's Queen Anne dining room chair covers. Maggie halted in mid-stride. She decided to investigate. If this was the perfect color, she'd have good news to report to Jean when this vacation was over. Maggie caught her breath, slid under the path's handrail and lowered herself to the edge of the lagoon bank. Gray, murky sand washed against the swamp's shore. She'd have to reach for the ribbon quickly or be pulled into the mud and salty water.

She leaned forward to retrieve the ribbon, pulled on the wisp of red floating above the surface, and lost her balance. Salty water engulfed her nostrils. She sputtered and jerked on the floating ribbon. A fierce tug brought the ribbon from the quagmire, and along with it, the dead body of a teenage boy. His pale blue eyes were wide open, and his light hair was saturated with blood and mud. Blood oozed from where his nostrils should have been. The ribbon slipped from around his neck and lay limp in Maggie's shaking hand.

" 'Gators! 'Gators!" she screamed. Crawling up the bank on her hands and knees, she stumbled, gasped, and screamed until she reached the handrail. Pulling with all her strength, she fled from the lagoon and headed down the trail, screaming and fighting back the pouring tears.

"Help! Help! Oh God, somebody," she howled as she approached the security gate. "An alligator has killed a boy, and it's after me." She gagged and flopped down on the curb by the gate. Slimy, swampy water trickled from her running shorts and ran in droplets down her legs.

The guard slammed the phone down in his office and ran to meet Maggie. He grabbed her by the shoulders. "A 'gator done ate a man in the lagoon? I knowed it would happen. I did. I did."

"There's a dead boy in the lagoon. About halfway down the trail. Please hurry. The tide will wash him away. Please. Please. I think an alligator got him. There was blood all over his face."

Maggie took a deep breath. She began to collect her wits. The heaving in her stomach subsided, but her legs were still shaking. "Call the police."

"Lady, I am the po-lice," the guard said. "I reckon the sheriff ought to know."

"Then call the sheriff. We need help here before the tide washes him away." He stepped inside the office and dialed the county sheriff.

17

A white Mercedes coupe pulled up to the gate. In the excitement, Maggie had not noticed its approach. The driver pressed an electric window button. "Are we being attacked by pirates? The screaming is making one hell of a noise on our quiet island." A slim, sandy-haired man, dressed for tennis in white shorts and polo shirt, extracted himself from the roadster.

Maggie pushed her soggy, plastered hair away from her face. A twinkle beamed in the man's shining blue eyes.

"Mister Heyward, sir." The guard came running out of his office. "I called the sheriff. This lady, she says she just saw a dead boy floating over in the marsh. Alligator got him. Go with me to take a look?"

"I'm John Pickney Heyward," the man said, as he extended his hand toward Maggie.

"Maggie Stewart." Maggie noticed black, sandy grit under her French manicure. She accepted his warm, firm grasp.

He turned his attention back to the guard. "You're serious, Joe? Dead? Watch my car, Maggie, and don't let anyone in or out of this gate. Come on, Joe, let's hurry. The tide's coming in."

Maggie stretched out on the hard asphalt road. Deep breaths began to calm her shaking body. Her mind's eye flashed back to the dead boy. She remembered a ribbon pretty enough to wrap a package, floating around the victim's neck. But not tied in a knot, or it wouldn't have come off in her hand. There had been enough blood to color the water. But only around the area of the head. The rest of the body seemed intact. She remembered seeing Birkenstock sandals by the water's edge. An approaching car jerked Maggie into the present. A rusty, green, 1964 Cadillac convertible slowly approached the gate from the main road.

"Where's Joe? He ain't supposed to leave his post," the driver said. "I can't wait. Tell him to pick up his share at the usual place. Seven tonight. Tell him I've got other deliveries and not to be late."

18

The Cadillac roared around the gate and down the road. "Wait," Maggie called. She realized she hadn't gotten the license plate number or his name. But how many Cadillacs like that would there be on the island? Besides, the driver seemed to know the guard.

"Joe, wait here for Sheriff Hammond," Maggie heard John Heyward say from across the road. "I'll take Maggie to the Meyers'. Tell the sheriff to come over there." Maggie jumped up and ran to meet the two men.

"What did you find?" Maggie asked.

"It looks like his head has been bashed in. Hey, don't get in my car. You smell like a three-day dead crab. We'll walk."

John propelled Maggie by the elbow and called over his shoulder: "Call the tennis club. Tell the pro to tell Alice we'll take a later court time."

Maggie stopped. She put both hands on her hips. "I am perfectly capable of finding my way alone." She stormed off in the direction of the Meyers' house. What a hell of a vacation this was.

"Wait," John called. He caught up with her, matching his stride with hers. "I'm not thinking. We don't find dead bodies on Seaward every day. In fact, no one's been killed here since the War of the Northern Aggression, that's what my Grandmother Pickney called it."

"You live on this island?"

"Since I was born. My great-grandfather owned the original plantation, Sea Island Cotton. I have an office on the mainland, but I spend most of my time here. Marilyn told everyone on the island that you'd arrive today. S.J.'s having people in tomorrow night to meet you."

"S.J. called earlier. I wonder if her plans will change now. This kid could be one of her students."

"No way. Her students wear the high-price brands and get their money from daddy's credit card. This poor guy had on off-brand jeans. Not the type S.J. cultivates."

"You sound as if you don't like her."

"She's trying to make this island into an exclusive golf and country club. Most of us want it to remain undiscovered. Since there's only so much property on the East Coast, that's probably a pipe dream. By the year 2025, more people will live on the coast than live in the world today."

"How do you know that?" In spite of her sogginess, Maggie felt comfortable walking down the road in a pink, misty twilight with a man who cared about something besides himself.

Maggie and John approached the front door to the Meyers' house. It was standing open. Maggie reached for the key in her pocket. Gone. The red ribbon dangled from her pocket and slipped down the side of her leg. Its sogginess felt slimy on her skin. Goose bumps once more covered her body. "I know I locked this door. I've lost the key."

"What's that?" John asked.

"The ribbon I found on the body. I must remember to give it to the sheriff. Does it look familiar?"

"No." He walked into the Meyers' house. "Anything missing? It looks okay in here."

"Maybe I didn't shut the door tightly. Perhaps the wind blew it open. Fix us a drink, if you don't mind. I could use one. I'll shower and be done in jiff."

The phone rang. Maggie jumped. She needed that shower and a drink to steady her ruffled nerves and calm her churning stomach. John grabbed the receiver and listened. "We'll be right there," he said.

"Now what?" Maggie asked.

"Sheriff Hammond wants us at the scene P.D.Q. Joe says he's raising almighty hell because you left."

Maggie stuffed the ribbon in her pocket, grabbed the extra key, slammed the door, and followed John down the road, her running shoes leaking briny water along the way.

Two

" Here's your gin and tonic," John said, holding out a glass to Maggie. "Sorry, no lime. You look better. Mud didn't match the blond in your hair."

"Thanks," Maggie said. "The shower washed away some of the stress, too. I haven't had time to stock the pantry. I see you found popcorn. At least Marilyn left that. Since the rain never came, let's take the popcorn and our drinks on the deck. Never waste a precious moment in the house at the beach when you can enjoy a wonderful starry night."

"Agreed."

John and Maggie strolled out the glass doors. He carried the bowl of popcorn and she balanced the drinks. They settled themselves on the old plastic deck chairs. Stars twinkled above the slapping waves, a soothing picture after the afternoon horror.

"Maybe I'll buy Marilyn and Greg nice wicker furniture. My thank-you present for the unlimited use of their house."

"Get something comfortable. Not stiff and new like they're selling everywhere," John said.

"I would. I love the old, soft, worn, lived-in cottage look. That's one reason I'm having career burnout. All my clients want the newest and latest. It's impossible to please most of them, and they all want what everyone else has. Human nature, I think."

"I haven't figured out human nature yet, but I think greed, power, control—the see-what-I've-got syndrome—are contributing factors. It's becoming more apparent, even on a remote island like Seaward. A lot of people here want a bridge, golf course, and all the trappings. Pardon the pun. I get really ticked. The wildlife refuge would become a way to attract customers to a new outlet mall. I bet they'd sell fake wicker at exorbitant prices."

"I wouldn't buy it," Maggie answered. "Of course, I'm able to get good deals at the Atlanta Furniture Mart."

They chuckled softly. Both reached for the popcorn at the same time. Maggie felt an unexpected tingle at the touch of John's hand, a feeling she had almost forgotten. The easy banter between the two continued for a while. Then both fell into a comfortable silence.

The dark night provided a luscious backdrop for twinkling stars and the ebbing of the tide.

John broke the silence. "A sand dollar for your thoughts."

"I guess I was thinking about this afternoon and my grilling by the sheriff. I understand why Hammond wanted the ribbon. Finger-prints and whatever else for the investigation."

"You can always find red ribbon. Let it go, Maggie." From the look on his face, Maggie knew that she'd better forget the ribbon. What difference did it make to John? She'd only known him a few hours. Maybe he's a moody man. That I don't need, she thought.

"Okay. Is the store still open? I need to stock up if I'm planning to eat while I'm here."

"The Kash and Karry open after dark?" John glanced at his watch. "It's two o'clock in the morning. We're not a twenty-four hour island."

"Did you say two? It seems early."

"Tell you what: Stock up tomorrow on the mainland. But meet me for lunch first at Aunt Patty's Cafe."

Maggie hesitated. She looked into his sparkling blue eyes. A year since Bob and no dates.

"Love to," she replied. "I'll catch the ten o'clock ferry and look in some antique shops before I meet you. After lunch, I'll do the store."

"Good. I'll help you load your supplies on the ferry."

They left the deck and walked to the front door. John took both of her hands and faced her. Then he kissed her on the forehead and walked out into a misty salt-air night. Maggie closed and locked the door. She placed her left hand on her forehead as she walked down the hall. Since childhood she'd used that gesture to symbolize sweet dreams in her head. In the master bedroom, she plopped onto the bed. Without putting on her night shirt, or even glancing at the stack of murder mysteries she planned to read during her vacation, she fell into a deep, hard sleep.

She woke with a start. It seemed only minutes since her head had dropped on the fluffy, down pillow. Sunbeams pouring through the sliding glass doors of the master bedroom were a relief after the bloody waves gushing through her dreams. The previous day's events sprang immediately to her mind. She stretched and took a long, deep breath.

The phone rang. Maggie answered on the third ring. It was Sheriff Hammond. He gave her a brief report and hung up before Maggie had a chance to ask questions.

The body had been identified. Michael McKay, a student visiting the island. He was applying for an internship with S.J. Styles. His head had been beaten to a bloody pulp. That was all he could tell her until the coroner's report came in. The soggy ribbon had no prints on it.

Maggie cradled the receiver before she turned over and looked at the clock. The coroner's report could take several days. If she was going to make the ten o'clock ferry to the mainland, she'd better get moving. Shopping, lunch with John, and the store fit the agenda for her first full vacation day.

When the coroner's report was ready, Maggie intended to see it. She fastened the last button on her denim jumpsuit, tied her hair back, and hurried down the front road to the ferry docks. Grasping the door key in her hand, she remembered that she needed to have another one made while she was in town.

The *Mary Grace* tooted the announcement of her departure. Several people gathered with Maggie to step aboard. All around her, people were talking about the murder. "Really horrible," she heard someone say. "It's gonna be worse than New York City if the bridge gets built. All kinds of hoodlums'll be coming over here."

Maggie pushed past the idle chatter and jumped on board. The ferry began to chug in the choppy sea.

Several people were standing or sitting in the cramped inside quarters of the little boat. Two men carrying briefcases, wearing coats and ties, stood out. They were undoubtedly on their way to mainland offices.

Maggie decided to stay topside. She inhaled the salty ocean air. Low-lying Seaward Island receded into the distance. Seaward Sound curved around the bend of the island. Sea gulls squawked their morning hunger cries.

Maggie saw a man stepping and swaying between briefcases, staring hard in her direction, lumbering toward her from below. He looked familiar. His cut-off jeans and faded yellow T-shirt contrasted with the office commuters. His beer gut prevented quick movement. Maggie stepped back, unsettled by the look in his eyes.

"Hey, wait," he called.

The *Mary Grace* pulled into the mainland dock with a sudden jolt. Maggie fell against the side rail. Passengers began to file out, pulling Maggie along with them. The man disappeared in the crowd, and Maggie dismissed him from her mind.

Rows and rows of rainbow-colored cottages filled the streets near the dock. The historic district, preserved by several societies of generous patrons, beckoned with its shops, restaurants, and significant artifacts. The bustle of the morning commuters waned. Maggie took a left and started up a steep hill. Townhouses appeared closer together. Imposing two-story bricks. Front doors closed, probably never used. Aristocracy closed to the world, she thought.

26

Maggie heard heavy footsteps close behind. She stopped to read a street sign. The footsteps behind her stopped. The streets were quiet. She looked back, but she saw no one. She quickened her pace. Two blocks ahead, a tour bus spilled passengers from its opening door. Maggie began to run. Footsteps pounded behind her. Another block and she would be in the middle of the tour group.

"Stop! Help! Someone is chasing me!" The sound of her voice bounced against the imposing brick. Maggie opened her mouth to scream again. Church bells from Saint Anthony's chimed eleven times. Maggie turned to see if she could spot a would-be assailant. Hands reached from behind and grabbed her. She screamed and fell to the ground on her knees.

"Are you always screaming?" John Heyward asked. "I was on my way to the ferry dock to meet you."

"It's...it's you! A man from the boat chased me up the street. I didn't see you come around the corner." Maggie's knees were shaking. Exhaust from the tour bus down the street caused her to gag. Her jumpsuit had dirt across the knee, and her long hair spilled from its navy ribbon.

"Did he threaten you? Where is he now? Should I chase him down?" John asked, his eyes darting.

"I didn't see him after I left the boat, but it had to be that man. I've seen him somewhere, before today. He looked familiar." She realized how hysterical she sounded and gave John an embarrassed smile. "I must be nervous because of the murder. I'm really more levelheaded than this."

John took Maggie's arm and helped her up. "Come on. Let's go over to Aunt Patty's Cafe and sort this out. Alice is meeting us there in a few minutes. She's always late."

"Your tennis friend?"

"Yes, she wants to meet you."

27

Maggie and John walked in silence. Walking quietly beside her, he had a calming effect.

"The man on the boat. I just remembered. I know where I've seen him."

John stopped in front of the cafe, a puzzled look on his face. "Where?"

"He was the one in the Cadillac, the one who left a message for Joe. Remember? The sheriff said his name was Leroy. He works at the saloon on Seaward."

"Leroy? Most people call him Toot. He's harmless. Born on Seaward. His great-grandmother was a midwife. His grandmother, Granny Jones, is a jewel. She takes care of all the locals on the island. He's had a few minor scrapes with the law, selling beer on Sunday, that kind of thing. He wouldn't be chasing you."

"He would be if he thought I saw him kill Michael McKay," Maggie shot back.

"Good point. Did Hammond call you this morning?"

"He gave me very little information."

They stepped into the coolness of Aunt Patty's Cafe. They were greeted by a big, grandmotherly woman whose smile matched her girth.

"Morning, John. You're late today. Of course, Alice isn't here yet. Your table is ready."

"Aunt Patty must make lots of money," Maggie commented, looking around. "This place is wonderful."

She and John were seated at what must have been one of the best tables. French doors opened to an English garden hidden from the street. Maggie could see herbs growing by the garden steps, and she smelled lavender on the breeze. The Victorian coziness and elaborate menu heightened the rumbling in Maggie's stomach. "You order for us," she told John.

28

"We should wait for Alice. She's anxious to meet you." John placed his menu on the table. "I talked to the coroner this morning. He's a friend of the family. Didn't mind sharing what he thinks.

"He thinks death had occurred a while before you found the body because rigor mortis had set in. He figures the kid was beaten to death, hit on the head repeatedly as he stood on the bank, and pulled into the lagoon after he died."

Maggie cleared her throat and took a sip of water. Nausea swelled in her stomach.

"Here I am. Ta da." Alice spread her arms out as if she were posing for the cover of a fashion magazine. "John, be a darling and order my coffee. I simply cannot function until my second cup."

Alice pulled a gold compact from her Gucci bag and checked her face. Thick makeup had begun to settle in the creases around her eyes. She dabbed at them with the powder puff. "John has told me all about you, Maggie. He said you babbled on until two this morning. How nice of you to get acquainted on your first vacation day."

Alice's huge diamond, set in a gold wedding band, sparkled in the mirror as she snapped the compact shut.

Alice was an older woman, probably in her forties, but still attractive. She was impeccably dressed, and every dark hair on her head was sprayed into place.

John studied his menu as if he'd never seen it before. "We were talking about the murder," Maggie told Alice. "Did you know Michael?"

"Of course not," Alice replied. "I just haven't the time to keep up with the strays that S.J. collects. She calls them art students. I'm not sure S.J. even knew him. He had impeccable recommendations, and S.J. was ready to take him in, sight unseen. She had an appointment with him at three o'clock yesterday, and he never showed. She's such a dear that way. I'm just hoping we don't have a crazy killer running loose on the island. That would absolutely ruin our chances to get state funding for an island bridge. That reminds me. John, after lunch you must come over to Ralph's office with me. I need to have those papers notarized before he returns. He called last night and said he'd be back on the late flight. He'll stay on the mainland and come out to the island on the first ferry tomorrow. Have you heard me, John? You're staring at the menu as if you'd never been here before."

The waiter approached the table, and Alice called out, "John and I will have our usual. What would you like, Maggie?"

A big gooey cream pie to push into that over-caked face, Maggie thought.

"Maggie, why don't we have the seafood chowder and Peter's special crab cakes? They're the best south of the Chesapeake Bay. Since you've never eaten here, I think you'd enjoy that," John said. "I'd enjoy a change, too. I've been in a rut lately."

"That sounds great." Maggie smiled at him.

Alice gave John a nasty look and kept talking. "And now, my dear, do tell me all about you. Marilyn says you're a decorator." Alice handed the menus back to the waiter. "Ralph and I may need you to put new carpet on the first floor of his office. I just don't have time to consider mundane details."

"Actually, I'm a designer. I draw up plans for rooms or major renovations," Maggie answered.

"Oh, I see," Alice said.

The food arrived and lived up to John's promise and Maggie's expectations. Alice excluded Maggie from the conversation whenever possible, and she seemed as relieved as Maggie was when lunch was over. John apologized to Maggie for not helping her grocery shop. He would go with Alice after lunch.

"We'll see you tonight at the party, won't we, John? John and I are going together, since Ralph couldn't be back." Alice placed her hand over John's.

"Bye. Thanks again." Maggie pushed the door to the restaurant open and felt the afternoon heat rise from the pavement into her face. It was stifling. John and a married woman. A possessive woman. Last night, she and John had had a wonderful time sipping wine, sharing popcorn and funny stories, and becoming friends. That woman had a strange hold over him. He was entirely different when he was around her. Her long red nails were probably silk-wrapped fakes, too. Maggie shook off the negative thoughts and heaved a sigh of relief. Alice wasn't part of her vacation plans.

A horse-drawn buggy stopped at the front of a Confederate statue. "Thank you for joining Lowcountry Tours," a college student said as he tipped his Confederate hat. Maggie became surrounded by a half-dozen or so people descending from the carriage, and she was carried along with the carnival-spirited tourists toward a battery guarding the tides of the Atlantic Ocean. Natives from surrounding islands plied their hand-woven sea grass baskets.

The baskets were a natural for Christmas presents. Maggie decided that she would buy several, store them in her attic, and hope that she'd remember them in six or seven months. As she reached into her pocket for money, she felt a tug on her arm.

"Lady, you stay out of my way. You never gave Joe my message. Messed up all my deliveries."

Maggie came face to face with Toot. His yellow T-shirt tugged against his pot belly. Maggie shivered. His stale breath assaulted her nose.

"And I sure as hell don't appreciate you telling that turkey Sheriff Hammond about me being there. You understand?"

And then he was gone. Maggie's enthusiasm was gone, too. She slumped on a bench overlooking the battery. Dancing sunlight spilled into the waters of the Atlantic Ocean. Too many fragmented details, and none could be tied with a red ribbon. Maggie made her way slowly up Prince Street to find the local grocery store.

Three

After putting away the groceries and tucking the extra key she'd had made into the kitchen drawer, Maggie hurried to shower and change into her "go anywhere" black linen dress. She took a deep breath and walked through a rusty, wrought iron gate to S.J. Styles' house. It loomed like an abandoned pink whale. Wouldn't it be lovely if it were a soft tan stucco melting into seat oats and looking as if it belonged? The double French doors, painted a deep black in harsh contrast to the house, had been thrown open, and Maggie stepped inside.

The foyer's vaulted ceiling opened to sky lights that filtered evening light through their glass. The emptiness of the expanse created a feeling of loneliness. Coldness seeped from a black tile floor. Images of a comfortable, inviting entrance popped into Maggie's head. Sea shades of turquoise and earthy hues of brown. A rich, warm hardwood floor. The hard, cold, black slate would go. This house could lend itself to milky pastels and soothing shades of sunny yellow. A Chinese needlepoint rug on the hardwood floor. Even a creamy entrance hall with a table filled with books and colors to pick up accents from the muted rug. Maggie shook her head. The only object in the empty foyer covered the entire left wall, an abstract painting. The painting belonged in a converted, New York Soho loft, Maggie thought.

Piano music, the tinkle of glasses, and laughter reached Maggie's ears. She followed the noise. The foyer spilled into a large, chalky white living room. Or maybe it was an art gallery. More abstract, meaningless artwork covered the walls. Track lighting glared from the ceiling and washed the paintings from peculiar angles. The gorgeous view of the Atlantic Ocean from glass that ran across the length of the room saved Maggie from screaming and running out the door. This place gave her the jitters. It could be so beautiful, she thought. Plump sofas, sumptuous textures, and subtle color would turn this into a magnificent beach cottage. Maggie could feel her spirit stretch out on a comfortable down-filled club chair facing the ocean. The perfect place to watch waves roll up the sandy beach.

"Maggie, it must be you. You're as beautiful as Marilyn said you were." S.J. broke away from an animated group and came toward her.

Marilyn, you owe me more than one for this, Maggie thought. She smiled brightly at S.J. It was obvious that Sondra Jean wanted everyone to know that she was an artist. She was almost as skinny as her gold cigarette holder, and she was the only person in the room smoking. Her Aztec patterned skirt swirled around bony ankles. The black, lacy camisole on her upper body was accented with a bright red shawl drawn loosely around her shoulders. The white room became a canvas for S.J. Styles.

"The entire island is buzzing about yesterday," she said. "Come join our conversation after you get a drink from the bar. Oh, check out my study and tell me what I should do. Take a peek in my studio down the hall. We're working with fabric and oils." S.J. breezed away.

Maggie stepped toward the bar in the hallway. She had no desire to tell her version of yesterday's horror. She stood in the middle of a mass of strangers. "Gin and tonic, please." She smiled at the young bartender, who must be one of S.J.'s students.

John walked up and touched Maggie's arm. "I'll have the same," he told the bartender.

"Sorry about lunch," he said to Maggie. "Alice likes to control the conversation."

Maggie wanted to ask him what he saw in that woman. Instead, she said, "The man on the ferry was Toot. He followed me down the street after I left you at Aunt Patty's. He told me to stay out of his way. Then he disappeared. It scared me. Are you sure he's harmless?"

"If it makes you feel better, tell the sheriff. I doubt that it's important. I've told you: Toot is as harmless as a newborn baby," John answered.

Before Maggie could answer, a red-faced, paunchy man with a fatuous grin pushed between them and rested his empty glass on the bar for a refill. "Hey, John," he said in a loud voice that stopped conversations all around him. "Which way we betting? Half the folks here say a jealous art student did it. The other half says the hoodlums that hang out at Dickie's saloon. Some are still saying alligators'll get us in our beds tonight. Ain't never heard anything like this." He took a large gulp from his refilled glass. "Oh, and a few think he was killed because of a drug deal that went sour."

Maggie slipped away from the two men and walked off down the hall.

How did John know what was important about this case? Was he hiding something that she should know? After all, there weren't a surplus of suspects: Toot, the gate guard, and maybe the sheriff thought she had a hand in it. And John. No, she wouldn't think that. His blue eyes looked sincere, especially when he focused on her. There was no rhyme or reason for the senseless killing of a young man. Unless drugs were involved. That's prejudice, she thought. All young people don't do drugs. Still, hadn't the man at the bar said something about drugs? And he certainly would know more about the island than she would.

Too many questions and no simple answers. It was Sheriff Hammond's job to find answers, not hers.

She stumbled into the room at the end of the hall. Easels, paints, and the aroma of paint thinner filled the light and airy room. Definite contrast to the rest of S.J.'s house, she thought. A colorful painting of the marsh, complete with alligators lurking on the bank, caught her eye. She was studying it when S.J. came in.

"Oh, Maggie, there you are," S.J. said. "I can't find Alice. Ralph came home early and he's looking for her. He's called twice. Has she been in here?"

"I haven't seen her. I was just admiring your studio. There's so much light," Maggie said. "It would be a wonderful place to compare the reaction of fabrics with response to light at different times of the day."

"Feel free to bring fabric over any time. The students and I are usually here all day."

"Thanks," Maggie said. "I've got to go now. I'll slip out the studio door and walk back on the beach. Hope you find Alice."

"Of course, dear. I'll give everyone your good-byes. See you soon."

Maggie turned the corner of the path and saw John put his arms around Alice. She ducked into the shadows of the dunes.

"You don't think she knows anything?" Maggie heard Alice ask.

Maggie held her breath. The pair passed without noticing her in the shadows. She didn't move until she heard the studio door close. Their words had been rather ominous. Who was "she" and what didn't she know? Was it about the murder or did it relate to their affair? But if they were talking about their affair, why wouldn't they be worried about what Alice's husband might know rather than some mysterious "she"?

Maggie moved on down the beach path, her head down, and her thoughts jumbled. A sea shell that was an unusual shade of pink caught her eye. She reached down and picked it up. She walked along, turning it over in her hand.

A log was half buried in the sand. Maggie didn't see it. She tripped and sprawled into the wet beach sand. Spitting, coughing, and sputtering, Maggie raised her head.

"Do you always try to look disheveled when you go out?" John's teasing voice carried over the sound of the waves.

Maggie jumped up and felt her ankle turn. She sat down hard. "I thought you and Alice were at the party."

"Too much smoke and noise for me," he answered. "I came out for a breath of fresh air. Saw you strolling down the beach and decided to join you. We've got to quit meeting like this. I don't mind if you shower before you see me." He sat in the sand next to Maggie, a broad grin on his face.

Maggie surveyed the damage from her fall. A few cuts and bruises. They matched the bruises from her fall in the swamp. Soon there would be no place on her body for a tan. Her linen dress was sandy, but not torn. "Where's Alice?"

"Ralph came home early from a business trip. He had jet lag and didn't want to come over. She left. Those two are having problems."

"I'll just bet they are," Maggie said.

"What do you mean?"

"Oh, come on," Maggie said, rolling her eyes. "It's obvious. You and Alice. If I know, then Ralph probably knows, too. This entire gossipy island knows."

"You don't like our tranquil sea island refuge?"

"You're not denying it?"

"I have nothing to deny. Alice was a friend of my sister, Catherine. She and Catherine were ten years older. They entertained sorority sisters with beach parties, probably in this very spot, every spring break. Mom and Dad would allow me to come on the beach for their late evening oyster roasts. Alice slipped me my first beer. I was really sick from chugging it quickly, so my parents wouldn't catch me. When I threw up all night, my parents thought the oysters were tainted. I never told them. Alice and I share a lot of memories. That's all."

"I'm not sure that she feels that way. She's extremely possessive toward you."

John sighed and looked out toward the sea. "My sister, Catherine, was killed in a boating accident a few years ago. Alice tried to save her. It's complicated. Alice has never forgiven herself. Are you okay?"

"Just a turned ankle. This is not the vacation I'd hoped for," Maggie said ruefully.

"I need to show you more of the island. I'll take you sailing this week."

Maggie responded with a delighted smile. "That would be great. I've watched the Carolina Regatta on Hartwell, the lake near Rosemont. I've never actually sailed, though."

"At last. I've found a willing sailing partner. Alice hates it. Wait until you see my boat. She's a beauty. While everyone else was memorizing 'Under the Spreading Chestnut Tree', I was reciting Richard Henry Dana, Jr. 'There is witchery in the sea, its songs and stories, and in the mere sight of a ship, and the sailor's dress…' "

"Let's go tomorrow," Maggie said.

John's smile was momentarily as eager as Maggie's, and then it faded. "Wait, I have to be on the mainland all day tomorrow. Mom's on the mainland in a nursing home. I visit her twice a week. She was never the same after Catherine died. Dad's last stroke left him paralyzed, and I became Seaward's caretaker. For nearly five years, I've been fighting to protect a habitat rather than build a golf course. Some of the islanders, especially Ralph, would like to see the land raped. And line their pockets with silver."

John gave Maggie a sheepish grin. "Sorry, I didn't mean to rave on. Anyway, I need to take care of the folks. Let's go Tuesday."

"Okay." Maggie looked out over the ocean. "I want to know more about Seaward. Marilyn told me that it was a refuge and camp for soldiers during the Civil War. Isn't there a big live oak tree on the other side of the island that the soldiers climbed to spot Union ships?"

"The Liberty Oak. There will be a big party at the oak while you're here. The local saloon owner is trying to raise money to upgrade their facilities and draw more tourists over here. I don't approve of the tourists, but I'm all for the party. Dickie, the saloon owner, will probably break even, and we'll all have a good time. What do you say we go together? Liberty Oak is the perfect place for a beach cookout. The islanders love any excuse for a party. There'll be more fun than funds. Dickie has delusions of grandeur. He's also the Meyers' maintenance man. If you need anything, I guess Marilyn told you to call him."

Maggie nodded. "I have his number. My ankle feels stiff. I need to get to the house and soak it."

"Come on, I'll walk you over there." He leaned over to help her up. His blue eyes stared intently into Maggie's face. His face moved closer. His lips were soft as he pressed them against Maggie's mouth. She gently tried to push away, but he held her tighter. A man who kisses like this doesn't commit murder, Maggie thought. The moon, stars, and a gently lapping tide created the moment. Maggie let herself relax into it. The shell slipped from her hand and fell gently into the sand, forgotten.

Four

Maggie stood in the darkness of her hallway and watched John walk back toward the party. It was only a kiss on the beach in the moonlight, she told herself, and it had been too long since she had been kissed. The magic was in the moonlight, not in the man, she said to herself sternly, but there was a stirring inside her that wouldn't go away.

His broad shoulders disappeared behind a dune, and Maggie stared at the spot where he had disappeared from view. Then she turned away in disgust.

"Get that silly feeling of moonlight and magnolias out of your mind," she said aloud. She wanted to believe that he was just friends with Alice. His story rang true, unless he'd told it often enough to make it believable. Maggie didn't need complications in her life. No more triangles for her. Never again. She flipped on the light switch and hobbled toward the kitchen. The red light was blinking on the answering machine. Maggie pressed the button.

"Call Sheriff Hammond when you come in," a stern voice instructed. "I'm on the mainland until the midnight ferry leaves. 555-6871."

Maggie dialed the mainland number. She mentally reviewed some of the things she wanted to talk over with him. She glanced around the kitchen while she waited for the sheriff to answer. Something was different about the room. She couldn't quite put her finger on it, but still...

The room was ergonomic, a term for the nineties, Maggie thought. On the marble countertops, a coffee machine, martini shaker, and a multitude of unused gadgets rested side by side. A mahogany humidor that belonged in the den sat between the cookbooks and the wine racks. She'd put the cigar box in its proper place tomorrow.

A deep male voice answered on the third ring. Her eyes continued to survey the room while she listened to Hammond.

"That boy was beaten to death," he said. "You there, Miss Stewart?"

Still gazing distractedly around the room, Maggie grunted to let the sheriff know she was listening.

"Anyhow," he said, "that about sums it up. The forensic report will give us more to work with. It won't be ready until Friday. About Toot, I've been talking to him. He said he followed you to the mainland. But he won't be bothering you no more. I put the fear of God into that lazy bastard. Pardon my French. He's just scared of the law. Thought you accused him of the murder. He ain't our man. I got some better leads."

He waited for a reply, but Maggie didn't answer. "Miss Stewart?"

"The key dropped out of my pocket at the murder scene, and now the one I lost is here on the table," she blurted.

"Well, honey, don't get yourself locked out," the sheriff said, apparently missing her point entirely. "Let me know if Toot bothers you again."

Maggie replaced the receiver. There was something else she'd planned to tell Hammond, but she couldn't remember. She had to find out how the key got on the table. After conducting a methodical search through the kitchen and finding only an empty plastic water bottle in the trash compacter, she began to walk through the rest of the house.

Maggie and the Meyers had spent countless hours planning this home. Husband and wife compromised as new purchases were made for a restful vacation spot. The atmosphere of the home pleased Maggie. A light palette of whites, and pastels, and cool hues of blue and green, and the palest of purples created a breezy tone.

Swivel club chairs, mobile enough to change positions from the summer ocean view to the cozy warmth of a winter fireplace, complemented the overstuffed, slip-covered sofa. The palest narrow sand-color strip in the sofa brought the focus needed to offset the sand-colored, cut pile carpet. Plenty of patterned scatter rugs over the plush carpet tied the colors in the rooms of the house together. Smooth cotton and nubby linen brought the feel of summer into every room. The vintage pillows on each end of the soda were an after-thought by Maggie that gave the room its pulled-together look. At the moment, pricey posters from art museums in different countries that Greg and Marilyn had visited adorned the walls. Maggie thought it a personal touch the couple would enjoy. Marilyn and Greg wanted to replace them when the budget allowed.

After two hours of looking over and under every piece of furniture, Maggie sat down on the king-size bed. The house looked the way she'd left it. Dust balls and sand were all Maggie found. She would track down the maintenance man at the beer joint tomorrow, talk to him about changing the locks. Maggie wasn't sure why, but she had an uneasy feeling that the person who left the ribbon at the murder scene had found her key, broken in, and was looking for the piece of ribbon Maggie had given the sheriff. No, she was being silly, jumping to paranoid conclusions, she decided. The ribbon at the scene could belong to a jogger who had lost it there earlier in the day. Then it would have nothing to do with the murder. But what if someone *had* broken in looking for the ribbon? How would that person know that Maggie had the ribbon? John knew. Had he told anyone else? There were a lot more questions about John than answers.

Maggie tucked herself under the down comforter and felt cool air blow across the room. She must have fallen asleep. When she glanced at the bedside clock, it beamed three a.m. back at her. She had pulled the covers around her tightly and had turned over to go back to sleep when she heard a noise at the front of the house. She sat up. Was the intruder returning? It sounded like scratching. A tree limb rubbing against the porch? Or was it the person who had been in the house earlier?

Maggie wasn't about to wait for a murderer to attack her. Quietly, she slipped from the warm bed and grabbed her terry robe. Sheriff Hammond was on the mainland. It would take ages for him to respond. She dismissed that idea immediately. The scratching at the front door got louder.

In total darkness, Maggie slowly crept along the front hall toward the door. Wiping tiny beads of perspiration from the top of her lip, she thought of calling the security gate, but she knew that by the time she got to the phone, the burglar would be inside the house. Would he beat her senseless, like Michael? What did she know that she shouldn't? Or did he think she knew more than she did?

Maggie stopped in front of the coat closet and weighed her options. The scratching had stopped. The attacker would be through that door any second. He didn't know she was waiting for him. "Here's to the fight of my life," she said quietly.

Gently turning the door knob of the coat closet, she reached in and grabbed the nearest makeshift weapon. Her pounding heart beat louder than the gentle closing of the closet door. She took a deep breath to calm her shaking hands. Poised by the front door, she knew it was time to make her move. In a steady, fluid motion similar to a tennis serve, Maggie lifted Greg's nine iron above her head. Almost at the same moment, she jerked the door open, turned the porch light on, and screamed.

A possum scooted off the porch and into the bushes. Maggie laughed with relief and a touch of hysteria. Just a possum looking for a midnight snack. Too many emotions were racing through her body. A course in stress management from the Rosemont Health Center would have been better than a Seaward vacation, she

44

thought. Before Maggie switched the porch light off, her eyes scanned the yard. The possum had crept out of the bushes and seemed to be wagging its tail and running toward her. A possum wagging its tail? Maggie rubbed her tired eyes and looked down. At her feet sat a furry Labrador retriever puppy. It plopped on its furry bottom and scratched its ear.

"You're not a possum," she said. "You are the cutest little dog I've ever seen." The puppy continued to wag its tail as it strolled into the house and directly back to the kitchen. Maggie closed the door, replaced the golf club in the closet, and followed the dog.

"Hey, pooch. You act as if you belong here. Marilyn and Greg didn't tell me about a dog. They would have asked me to feed and care for you. What's your story? Shipwrecked and washed in with the tide? Dumped as garbage along the road? Look, pooch, no. Your name is Possum. Okay, Possum, I don't have your kind of food. Would you settle for a turkey sandwich? We'll share. You look too well fed to be a stray. I'll help you find your home tomorrow."

Maggie busied herself with a middle-of-the-night version of a doggie gourmet meal. Possum, a female, Maggie noted, agreed that it was indeed better than any previous meal. The dog pushed the cereal bowl around the tile floor with her nose and gulped every last morsel.

"Enough for now. We don't want to give you a tummy ache. I don't even know if you're housebroken. You'll have to spend the night on the deck. I'll close the gate and give you a beach towel to sleep on. This isn't my house, you know. Carpet shampoo is not an item I normally buy at the store."

Possum wagged her tail and followed Maggie to the door. Maggie settled the dog and brought a bowl of water in case the dog got thirsty before she woke up. After locking up for the third time, Maggie padded back down the hall wondering what she was going to do with her new responsibility. Look in the Yellow Pages on the mainland for a vet and find out how to advertise a lost dog, she decided.

She caught sight of a conch shell on a side table, and suddenly she remembered a kiss on the beach that took her breath away and a pretty pink shell she had dropped in the sand. She was too restless now to sleep. She quickly threw on shorts and a shirt and headed toward the beach for a walk.

Possum was curled in a furry ball, asleep, with a full tummy.

The tide had turned. Ocean covered the spot where she and John had been sitting. Maggie walked up the beach a few yards looking for the shell. A futile attempt, but why not look? It might make a nice souvenir of this romantic night. Finding that one shell was like finding a needle in a haystack. It was gone, washed away to another world.

That settled, Maggie began to walk back down the beach. Her ankle didn't throb. It had been just a mild sprain, apparently, and she decided she could jog again. But she would jog down the beach in tomorrow's daylight. No more marshlands on this vacation.

S.J.'s studio light was on. She must be working late. Creative people sometimes worked all night and slept all day.

Maggie noticed a boat as she turned into her walkway. Fishermen out early for the morning catch, she thought. She had not heard a motor. The sixteen-foot Boston Whaler was anchored a few yards from shore. Maggie squinted into the gray mist on the ocean. The sun had begun to rise. Aboard the boat, two men were yelling at each other. One of the voices sounded like Joe, the guard from the gate, but she couldn't get a good look at the men. They were probably debating the best fishing spots for the day, she decided.

Maggie yawned. She had not planned a sunrise viewing this morning. Her body proclaimed it was still the middle of the night. She would slip back under the covers for a few more hours. She had plenty to do, and finding a home for Possum was first on her agenda.

As she pulled the covers over her head, she dreamed of a yacht sailing on the ocean. A handsome crew member who bore a strong resemblance to John handed her a drink in a beautiful pink shell and waited to hear what else she might want from him.

Five

" She's healthy," the vet declared. "She definitely belonged to someone. Must be lost, but I haven't heard any reports of lost dogs lately. She'll be a fine pet for you, if no one claims her."

Dr. Franks leaned down and scratched Possum behind the ears. He was rewarded with an enthusiastic wag of Possum's tail.

Maggie started to thank him for the house call, but he waved her thanks away.

"I'm glad I was on the island today. I needed to check the Perkins' horse. Had colic for two days. I'd better go see what we're gonna do with that mare," Dr. Franks said. "Start Possum on puppy food and make sure she stays on the heart worm medicine. It's bad around here. The Greens lost their collie to heart worms a few weeks ago."

He looked down at Possum and smiled. "She sure likes you, Ms. Stewart."

Possum was sitting on Maggie's feet, chewing on the tassel of her loafer. When Maggie tried to get the tassel out of Possum's mouth, the dog gave Maggie's hand a happy lick.

"How old do you think she is?" Maggie asked. "And what breed is she? Do you know anyone, anyone at all, who wants a puppy?"

"That's one of the prettiest yellow Labs I've ever seen." Dr. Franks said. "Look at the shape of her head. Long eyelashes, too. She's about five to six months old. She can be spayed if you don't want puppies. She's housebroken; she knew what to do when I took her out in the front yard."

"Puppies? I don't even want this one." Maggie picked Possum up and rubbed her head. "It's okay, poor baby, we'll find you a good home."

"Looks to me like she already has one," the vet said with a grin. "Call my office on the mainland if you have any problems."

Maggie closed the door, sat on the sofa, and rubbed the dog's silky coat. "You couldn't have been lost for very long. Maybe some family went back to Ohio or somewhere, and you had strayed and…"

Possum interrupted by putting her front paws onto Maggie's chest and licking her on the face. She smiled, in spite of herself. "You're a sweetie pie-pie," she said, and then added in disgust, "Now I'm talking baby talk to a dog."

The phone rang, and Maggie put Possum down. The dog stared up at her adoringly. "Maybe that's Sheriff Hammond calling to let me know they've found you a home. I've spent the whole morning calling around. Maybe S.J. will take you. She seemed interested."

But it wasn't the sheriff. The low, masculine voice on the phone made her heart beat just a little faster. "Hello, John. Do you want a Lab puppy? She's beautiful. I found her at my door last night after you left."

Maggie continued to chat with John while Possum whined to sit on her lap. She picked the dog up. "So I don't know a dog from a possum. Quit laughing. But, yes, it's funny. Of course I still want to go sailing. Okay. I'll see you tomorrow. Ask your friends if they want a dog. You take care, too. Bye."

She hung up the phone and smiled down at Possum. "Miss Possum Pie, you've got to stay here while I go to the Kash and Karry to get puppy food just for you. And a doggie bone if you're good while I'm gone. I've got to find the handyman saloon owner, get him to mow the grass. Maybe he'd like to have you. Do you want to be a bar stool doggie?"

Possum whined and licked Maggie's hand. "Don't do that," she scolded. "I absolutely will not get attached to a dog." She patted the dog's head and placed a water bowl on the floor by the sink. "Take care of the place, and I'll be back soon." Maggie closed the kitchen door and went out to Marilyn's Volvo.

As she sped down the road toward the security gate, she thought about the guard, Joe. Perhaps he'd seen Possum yesterday. She stopped the car. Joe came out when she approached the gate.

"Morning. Nice day. Glad to see you driving and not running after 'gators today." Maggie ignored the remark.

"You must be quite a fisherman. I saw you early this morning on a boat with a buddy."

"Me? Oh, no, not me. I'm a-working all the time now. The other man quit, and we can't find a replacement. I've been a-working full time. I don't fish much anyway. You have a nice day." He tipped his hat and turned to walk away.

"Wait a minute," Maggie called after him. "I just wanted to ask if you'd seen anyone looking for a lost puppy. I found one, and I'm looking for her owner."

"There's more dogs around here than you can shake a stick at. Some tourist musta put it out on the ferry. They do that all the time. We got a bunch of wild cats on the island, too. You get scratched by one of them creatures, you get mighty sick."

"Thanks for your help," Maggie said, and she drove on before she remembered she wanted to ask him about the message from Toot. She shrugged and kept driving. He'd probably just deny that, too.

The Kash and Karry, a small metal building with a tin roof, came into view about two blocks from the gate. The parking lot was compacted sand. A lone rusty shopping cart tilted sideways against the door. Maggie walked around the cart and entered the store.

She was greeted immediately by a painfully thin, gray-haired man who wore an eager-to-please smile. "Mornin'," he said in a high-pitched voice. "You must be Miss Marilyn's friend. She told us you'd be coming. What can we do for you? The Kash and Karry is at your service."

"I've found a lost dog. Has anyone reported her missing?"

The man shook his head.

"I need to find her a good home. Until I do, I'd better buy some food for her. Where's your dog food aisle?"

"Come on back. I'll show you where it is. If there's something you want that we don't have, I can order it from the mainland. It'll come in this afternoon on the *Mary Grace.*"

"You've got a great selection," she said. She picked up a dusty bag. "It looks like it's, um, been here for a while."

Maggie picked out dog food, lamb and rice for puppies, a red leather collar, a leash, and a very large, taupe-colored dog bed filled with cedar shavings. Then she added a bag of dog bones to the pile. She paid for her purchases, and the friendly grocery man helped her carry them to the car.

"I just talked to Joe at the gate. He says that he doesn't fish. Do you?" Maggie asked.

The grocer looked surprised. "Joe, not fish? He was a-pulling your leg. He's the best blue fish waterman we got on this island. Reckon he didn't want to share his secret spots with you. Did you come down to fish? I have a boat and would be glad to take you out."

"Thanks, but I'd just like to find the time to relax on the beach. I've got to find the saloon now. The handyman for the Meyers works there. I think the phone's been disconnected."

"He probably didn't pay his bill," the grocery man said, shaking his head. "I don't know even how he stays in business. Nobody wants his stale beer. Be careful when you go in there. 'Course, in daylight you ain't gonna have to step over too many drunks. Have a good day now."

He closed the car door, and Maggie left to find the handyman. From the store, it was a short drive to the bar.

When Maggie stepped through the door of the Red-Eye Bar and Grill, she had to wait for her eyes to adjust to the gloom. When her vision cleared, the first thing she noticed was a commercial phone that had been ripped off the wall. The hole made an appropriate image for the entire ambiance, or lack thereof.

It was clear the Red-Eye had stood on this spot for decades. She had heard that the bar had claimed many different names over the years but had always served the same strong spirits. Everything looked so dusty and worn, Maggie half-expected to see a sign on the wall that said "George Washington slept here." Instead, she saw a crude, hand-painted sign:

Fund Raiser Saturday Liberty Oak
To help buy paint and
Make the Red-Eye Red again. $5.00

A flashing beer sign dangled behind the massive oak bar. At some point, that bar must have been impressive. Now, it was dirty and scratched.

Maggie climbed on a plastic-covered stool. "Water, please," she said to a bartender who looked as worn and scarred as the bar.

The room stank of sweaty bodies and stale smoke. The Red-Eye needed more than a coat of paint.

Maggie decided she needed something stronger than water. "Beer. In the bottle, please," she said. She hoped a bottle would be cleaner than the glasses lined up behind the bar appeared to be.

The bartender peered at her through glasses specked with dust and dandruff. "You lost?" he asked. "Got a flat?"

"No, I came looking for you. I'm Maggie Stewart. I'm staying at the Meyers' this week."

Dickie Diamond popped the top off a can and slammed it down on the bar in front of Maggie. "This is all we got until the *Mary Grace* comes in this afternoon," he said.

Maggie took a swig of the beer, which wasn't nearly cold enough. "I've been trying to call you. I need some work done at the Meyers'."

"Oh, that. Well." He glanced at the gaping hole in the wall, where the pay phone dangled from a black cord. "If I turn it right side up, sometimes I can dial out. The phone man said he'd be over about Friday." He made a rumbling sound that might have been his version of a chuckle, and shook his head.

"My girlfriend, Sally Jo, did that. She gets jealous sometimes if I talk to other women at the bar. She thinks I'm quite a ladies' man when she's not looking. Wants me to marry her, but I'm in no hurry to settle down." He looked Maggie over. "Are you married?"

Maggie stiffened, and she felt her face flush. "As I told you, I came to hire you to do some work for me at the Meyers' house," she said, making no effort to hide her anger and revulsion.

Dickie Diamond shrugged. "You're a pretty woman," he said, "all alone in a bar. Can't blame a man for gettin' ideas. What you want me to do?"

"Mow the grass. Wash the windows. And help me get the locks changed. I may also need a few other chores done this week."

"I can handle that," he said. "Why you need to change the locks? Ain't been a robbery on Seaward since I can remember. Nobody around here locks their doors."

"I lost a key the day that Michael McKay was murdered."

"Now I remember. You're the lady that found his body. You heard anything about who might have done it? Did one of those art students kill him, you think?"

"Anybody on the island could have done it," she said. "I wonder who had the motive."

"You're talking like one of them Perry Mason reruns. You ever watch it?"

"No, I guess my mind just works that way. Did Michael ever come in the Red-Eye?"

"Once, the day he was killed. By hisself. Acted like he was waiting for somebody. He seemed jumpy. None of my regulars liked him. 'Course, they don't like none of them mainlanders that S.J. drags in. She don't bring them students here no more. Said we didn't have enough local color to paint. Don't need her no how. I'm raising the money and painting this place myself."

"Did Michael meet anyone here?"

"Naw. He drunk a few beers and left. A beeper went off on his watch, and he paid and left. Maybe he was killing time 'til he had to be somewhere. I never talked to him."

"Is there a store on the island that sells red satin ribbon?" Maggie asked.

"Red ribbon? You don't need to buy that. The volunteers at the Mainland Fire Department have boxes of it. They'll give you as much as you want. They got it for some kind of anti-drug program for the local high school. I got a couple boxes in my storage room. My buddy Toot Sweet got it for me. We gonna use it to decorate for the fundraiser Saturday. You wanna buy a ticket?"

"I'll get one later this week. John and I may come together. Here's two dollars for the beer," Maggie said, getting up from the sticky plastic seat. "One more thing: I've found a lost puppy. If you hear of anyone missing a yellow Lab, tell them I've got it. Maybe you could post a sign on your wall. Come by as soon as you can, please. That lawn is starting to look pretty bad."

Maggie grabbed her purse and fled as quickly as she could without running. The fresh salt air at the front door smelled divine. She took a last, uneasy glance over her shoulder and saw a short, stocky man slink out of the shadows in the back of the bar. She recognized him instantly. He was staring in her direction with open hostility.

Just before she stepped outside, she heard the man curse under his breath to the bartender and say, "What's that nosey broad doing here?"

Maggie hesitated outside the open door and caught Dickie's answer.

"She wants me to do maintenance at the Meyers' house. Must be paranoid about that murder. Kept asking me questions. Is she the one told Sheriff Hammond that you was over near the marshes, Toot?"

"Yeah. Got me in all kinds of hell. She better leave me be," the short man growled.

"You ain't in no trouble, are you, Toot? I mean, you don't know nothing about that murder, do you?"

" 'Course not. Come on and help me unload the supplies from my Caddie. I gotta help Mama at the produce co-op this evening. We got extra beer for the party Saturday night. Hope we make money. You ain't paid me in two weeks."

"You ain't worked much in the last two weeks," Dickie snarled back, as the men walked toward a back room.

As Maggie quietly walked away, she heard something that made her stop in her tracks.

"Where's them boxes of ribbon that was on the floor?" Dickie asked. "I thought we'd decorate with them down at Liberty Oak."

"Boxes of ribbon?" Toot sounded baffled. "Oh, the ribbon from the fire department? I gave them to that art teacher. She said her class was doing some kinda texture paint thing. We don't need ribbon. That's kinda girlie anyway."

Six

"Could this all just be coincidence?" Maggie asked herself aloud, sitting on the nubby linen sofa and scratching an ecstatic Possum behind the ears. There was a red ribbon at the murder scene. Was it a message left behind by the killer? The art students and Toot Sweet had access to red ribbon. For that matter, so did anyone who had been by the Mainland Fire Department.

"Possum, what have I missed? Have I seen something that makes the murderer think I know who he is?"

From Maggie's lap, Possum gave a hefty puppy sigh, closed her eyes, and drifted into a contented nap.

"After all that good puppy food, I'd think you'd want to go to sleep in your new bed. But no. You want to curl up in my lap. What will we do when you weigh seventy pounds? You'll flatten my leg bones. Oops. Bad thinking. I'm finding you a new home, remember?"

Possum continued to make contented puppy sounds in her sleep.

This murder couldn't be tied together in a neat package, not with any color of ribbon, Maggie thought. Maggie began to think about the victim. He'd been beaten to death with a passionate anger. Did the coroner think he'd been strangled with the ribbon? Who would want to do such a violent act to a guy in the prime of his life? Maggie shuddered. Possum whimpered in her sleep.

The list of suspects gets longer every time I set foot out of this door, Maggie thought. Dickie Diamond was so desperate to save the bar, he might kill someone just to bring morbid tourists to the island. No, that's not a motive. What about Joe? He was a competent security guard, but he'd lied to her about fishing and tried to keep her away from the marsh the day she found the body. But what kind of motive did he have? Drugs? Money? Sex?

Maggie continued to run a list of suspects through her mind. Possum was content to sleep on her lap. The sun faded behind the house, and twilight cast purple shadows on softly lapping ocean waves.

If you were making a list of suspects, you had to include Alice, Maggie decided. No, that's not fair, she thought. She's got a strange hold over John, but that's all. "I'm just upset that he didn't call this afternoon," she admitted to the sleeping puppy.

Who else could have a motive? Any one of the art students could be guilty, she thought. Jealousy was a great motive. Toot Sweet was near the scene but probably not smart enough to have a motive.

Could it have been a random crime?

"Well, Possum, we haven't heard from John, so I'd better think about dinner."

The phone rang. Maggie set Possum on the floor and padded across the room to answer it. It must be John, she thought, and the idea brought a smile to her face. "Ah, speak of the devil and he conjures himself up. Hello?"

"Maggie Stewart?" a deep, husky voice asked. "I have information for you about Michael McKay. Meet me at the Liberty Oak. One hour. Be there."

The connection went dead in Maggie's ear. It had sounded like a hoarse, male voice, but maybe it was disguised. This confirmed that she knew more than she thought she did, Maggie decided. Maybe this was the person who had found the key in the swamp and entered the house. "Guard the place, Possum," she said as she grabbed her car keys.

She left all the lights on and checked the lock on the door before she jumped into Marilyn's white Volvo.

The Liberty Oak grew near the edge of the north harbor. Some islanders claimed it had been there for hundreds of years. Spanish moss hung on massive branches, creating an umbrella over the shell-scattered beach. The tree had been a meeting place for American Revolutionary soldiers, and a place to restock supplies for the Civil War Underground Railroad. In recent history, it had become a gathering place for island oyster roasts.

Maggie stepped on the accelerator and followed the small, green signs down the dirt road toward the tree. The sky was clear, and a spring full moon cast a glowing light through the branches of the tree. Waves were lapping over the sand. Maggie parked near the tree and stepped out of the car.

"Anybody here?" Maggie called. Silence. Not even a breeze from the ocean stirred the night air. She walked past the oak and sank her feet into the sand on the beach. The huge, yellow moon glowed so brightly, it was almost like day on the sand. Lively little ghost crabs pranced along the beach. Her eyes wandered down to the water, but she saw no one. A few more minutes and she would leave. Paper cups and beer bottles littered the oyster pit on the beach. Maggie leaned over the grate to pick up the trash. If Dickie and his friends were partying here, they should clean up their mess, she thought.

A single, sharp swish flew past her right ear. She reached up to brush a mosquito away, and her hand hit a piece of driftwood. She turned. The driftwood came at her again, barely missing the side of her head. Spinning around, she came face-to-face with her assailant. He was dressed from head to toe in black. A silvery mask covered his face. He held the piece of driftwood above his head, poised to strike again. Quickly, Maggie grabbed a beer bottle and smashed it against the tree. She waved its jagged edge at the man.

"Don't come near me," she shouted.

"Stay out of our island's business," the black-clad figure said in a hoarse whisper before turning and fleeing into the swampy grass beyond the Liberty Oak.

Maggie breathed a sigh of relief and dropped the bottle. Her heart was pumping hard, and her body began to shake violently.

Maggie ran back toward the car. Bushes moved. Birds screeched. She stopped and listened. He was coming back! She heard the sound of footsteps. She wished that she still had the bottle. Before she could decide which way to run, Dickie Diamond came crashing through the branches of the Liberty Oak.

"Yo, Maggie," he called. "Did Toot get the mess on the beach cleaned up? We got to be ready by Saturday." The expression on his face turned to one of concern. "What's a matter? You crying? What you doing here at this time of night anyhow?"

Maggie began to explain between sobs. When she had finished, she asked, "Did you see him as you were coming in?"

"Ain't seen nobody. You say he wasn't tall as me? Dressed in black, you say, like maybe Darth Vader?"

"That's a great description," Maggie said between sobs.

"Come on. We're going to walk down the beach and look for this dude."

"Shouldn't we call the sheriff?"

"We'll call him after we nab the bastard. You coming?"

Maggie ran to catch up with Dickie. They trudged along the beach in silence. The tide was coming in. Any footprints would have been washed away. The dunes seemed undisturbed.

"His voice didn't sound like Toot Sweet's," Maggie told Dickie. "It was hoarse, scratchy."

"Toot's harmless," Dickie said.

"Was that his Cadillac parked at your place when I left?"

"That old piece of crap? Toot's brother, Clyde, won it in a poker game. Couldn't make it run and gave it to Toot. He's good with cars. Got it running a couple of months ago. It's his pride and joy. Says he's gonna get the rust off. When he's not at the Red-Eye, he's working for Alice Randolph. Thinks she's gonna give him the money. Ha! Alice and Ralph ain't never give nobody nothing."

Dickie stopped talking and pointed toward the dunes. "Looka there."

Sea oats had been trampled in the dunes. A piece of red ribbon spiraled across the sand.

"That's like the ribbon that was near Michael," Maggie told Dickie. "Did he mean to tie it around my neck after he killed me? Dickie, you saved my life. He heard you coming and ran." Maggie grabbed Dickie and hugged his neck. "Leave the ribbon here. We don't want to touch the evidence."

"Just don't let it get around that you hugged me," Dickie said. "Sally Jo don't cotton to my hugging other women."

"I'll hug her, too," Maggie shouted, running down the beach toward her car. "Come on, Dickie. We've got to get in touch with Sheriff Hammond."

Dickie puffed after her as fast as he could. His beer belly jiggled with every step. "You know," he yelled after her between labored puffs, "you're either a marvel or your marbles are loose. I haven't decided which yet." Dickie reached the car a dozen steps behind Maggie.

"Get in," Maggie said. "I'll take you back to your truck after we talk to the sheriff. I hope he's not on the mainland tonight."

"Hey, I hear a boat. Listen," Dickie said.

He and Maggie peered through the branches of the Liberty Oak. "That looks like the boat I saw in front of the beach house. The same two men are sitting in the bow," she said.

"I ain't never seen that boat before. Thought I knew every boat on this island. One of them guys must be the man in black. The other one just picked him up," Dickie whispered. "Wait 'til they've gone to start the car."

Dickie and Maggie eased into the Volvo and waited until the boat's sound was a distant purr. Maggie started the car and kept her eyes on the road.

"I hope the sheriff knows more than I do," she said. "He told me he had some leads. I know now that the ribbon is important. Maybe there'll be some prints on it."

"This is better than TV," Dickie said. "Never thought I'd be helpin' the cops. They always after me about my liquor licenses. Guess stranger things have happened. I'm gonna change your locks tomorrow. Don't want nobody getting you again."

Maggie shuddered. She realized what a close call she'd had. She glanced in the rear-view mirror. A navy blue Mercedes sedan was coming up behind her. It was going at least eighty in the dark night, and it was almost on her bumper. The driver honked the horn and pulled around the Volvo without slowing down.

"That's Alice Randolph, coming from the direction of Mister Heyward's. Reckon what she's doing at his house this time of night?" Dickie said. His wicked grin said he thought he knew exactly what she was doing there.

Maggie didn't answer. She didn't need to comment. Now she knew why she had not heard from John.

She pulled the car into the Meyers' driveway. The house was dark. She thought that she'd left lights on.

"I'll run in and call the sheriff," she said, racing ahead of Dickie. "Maybe he'll meet us here and we can all go back to the Liberty Oak together. He'll want to see the scene of the assault."

Maggie took the front steps two at a time. She was excited; fingerprints on the shiny ribbon might give the sheriff a suspect, or even catch the killer.

Maggie turned the key in the lock, opened the door, and turned on the hall light. She put her hand over her mouth. Only a hurricane could have done this much damage. Tables had been overturned. Seat cushions from the den were scattered across the floor. Every drawer in the house had been emptied. Nothing seemed to be broken. And then she realized: Possum wasn't in the house. Someone had done a thorough search and left a mess. They had either taken the dog or scared it away. Maggie kicked her way through the mess to the telephone. The line to the sheriff's office was busy.

She looked around for Dickie and realized he hadn't followed her inside. "Dickie," Maggie called, as she walked to the front door. "Someone's broken in again. Dickie..." Dickie wasn't in the car. He was running down the road toward the security gate.

After what seemed like hour to Maggie, a 1992 cobalt blue Ford truck pulled into the Meyers' driveway. A .22-caliber rifle protruded from the dashboard gun rack. Deputy Watson extracted himself from the seat. Maggie heard the truck and walked to the door. At last, the sheriff had finally sent someone. It had taken forever to get through to him. She had started putting the house back together.

Nothing seemed to be missing. One brief case with design projects had been ripped open. The burglar had spent considerable time going over her notes and swatches. He was definitely interested in her.

"Come in," she said as she opened the door. "I'm Maggie."

"Deputy Watson."

"Thank you for coming. After I called Sheriff Hammond, I remembered something else. Should we go back to Liberty Oak? Dickie disappeared, but I can show you where we left the ribbon."

"We've got an APB out on Diamond," the deputy said. "We'll catch him and check out his story. He's had quite a few minor altercations with the law. All them guys that hang out at the Red-Eye are a bunch of no-goods. Don't think a one of them ever did a decent day's work. Don't you let this bother you. Just stay away from that bunch of losers. Hammond said that you had some other information for us?"

Jethro Watson reached for the black comb in his shirt pocket. It rested behind a pack of Marlboro filters. He ran the comb through his greasy hair and smiled at Maggie. She led him into the living room, and he situated himself on the comfortable linen sofa. The heels of his black snake-skin boots were leaving smudgy marks on the pale scatter rug. "All them people that hang out at the Red-Eye are scairt of the law," he said. "Bunch of no-goods. Anyway, we'll check his story."

"I forgot to mention that we saw a boat after my attacker fled. Dickie will back me up on this. Maybe that's how the attacker got away so quickly. Anyway, I wanted you to know. It's the same boat that I saw anchored in front of this beach house the other night. Aren't you going to write this down?"

"Excuse me, little lady, but what's a boat got to do with this? This is an island. Without a bridge. Boats come and go around here all the time."

"I know that," Maggie said firmly, "but this one was different. It didn't have Marine numbers on the bow. It's probably not registered with the state. Please check it out."

"Without numbers, how are we supposed to check? You didn't see it up close. Probably had its registered numbers on the back. Might have been Woody Cecil's fishing boat. He usually comes in about that time every night. Ties up at Markley's Landing. You oughta go over there and buy some fresh fish. Mighty good eating."

"Just tell Hammond about the boat. I think it's important. I'll go over to the landing and see if I recognize any of the boats moored there. Are you going to Liberty Oak for that ribbon?"

"Now, little lady…"

Maggie's eyes blazed. "It's Maggie, not little lady."

"Now, Miss Maggie, I know you're upset about the murder, your break-ins, the attack on you and all that. And didn't you say something about a missing dog that's not yours? I know it ain't been easy since you come here. We gonna get it all straightened out. I'll tell Ham about the boat. He's been sheriff in these parts nigh onto thirty years. He ain't gonna cotton to nobody telling him how to do his job, especially a lady. He don't need no help. If I was you, I'd be worried about stealing that ribbon from the murder scene, although you did give it back. I'd also watch out who I run around with. Dickie and Ham ain't exactly friends, you know."

"Thank you for coming. And don't bother about Possum. I'll find her." Maggie rose and started toward the front door.

"You got a missing possum, too? I'd better add that to my report." Watson gave Maggie a wicked leer.

"I've summarized the events for Hammond and have now told you everything I know," Maggie said, not bothering to hide her contempt. "I expect to hear from you after the capture of my assailant. He shouldn't be hard to find on a small island without a bridge."

Watson walked through the front door. "Well, don't worry your pretty little head no more. Enjoy the vacation. Nothing could be finer than to be in Carolina." He continued to whistle the tune as he opened his truck door.

Maggie slammed her front door with a bang that rattled the walls.

"Little lady, my ass," she said. "I'll go find Possum myself."

Seven

While Maggie was dealing with Dickie and Deputy Watson, John Heyward was having problems of his own. Namely, Alice Randolph. He tapped his pen on the desk several times and looked at the phone, but he knew it would be a while before he could call Maggie.

"Alice," he said as he stood up and walked over to the French doors in his study. He wanted to bolt through the door and run screaming into the night. Instead, he took a deep breath and faced Alice.

"What exactly is it that you want from me?"

"Darling, how could you talk to me in that tone of voice? You have completely misunderstood. I don't want you to do anything dishonest. It's just, you know, Ralph and I must have that bridge built from the mainland. We've put all of our eggs in this basket, so to speak. The property we own out here is worthless unless we get the bridge built and have all those vacation-seeking tourists pouring onto Seaward. We can have golf courses, restaurants, houses, condos. People are spending megabucks on Kiawah. We could have that here. Why won't you listen to reason? All you have to do is talk to the county commissioner. He respects you. He could get the development plan moving. By this time next year, this God-forsaken island would be booming. And so would we."

"More likely, it would look as if it had been hit by a scud missile. Or worse. Alice, I am not going to sell out and lose the last slice of heaven on the Atlantic coast."

"You don't need the money!" Alice screeched. Her high-pitched scream echoed through the halls of the Heyward Plantation. "You've never known what it's like to lose everything," she sobbed.

"Ralph and I are counting on this project. You have known me since we were children. Where is your loyalty to friends who love you and need you now?"

"Oh, Alice. If it were only that simple. You can't begin to understand the implications."

"Implications, hell!" Alice sobbed. "All I know is that if you don't help us get the bridge built to this crummy place, then we'll just find someone else to do it. You are going to be very, very sorry that you lost out on this deal." Alice snatched her purse off the floor.

"Wait, Alice, don't leave in such a huff. We can try to talk rationally about it. You know I have a meeting next Tuesday with the County Board. Let's leave it at that."

"But I don't know what you're going to say to them. We've got to have that bridge. We must sell this island land. You know that. Ralph and I have everything tied to this deal."

"Please, please, Alice, calm down. This is getting us nowhere."

"And nowhere is where you're going to be if you keep trying to play Mr. Green Earth and all that crap. No, don't try to pat me on the head and say this is going to be okay. It isn't. Unless you help us to get that bridge built and turn this mosquito-infested hell-hole into a tourist paradise."

"I'm sorry, Alice. Truly. But I think you'd better leave. I'm certain that Ralph doesn't know you're here. I'll talk to him before Tuesday."

"You just do that. And go straight to hell!"

Alice placed her leather bag on her shoulder and stormed through the house to the door. John heard the heavy door slam and tires screech in the driveway. He walked over to the bar and poured himself a strong single malt Scotch with a splash of water.

The cook came through the study door with a puzzled look on her face.

"I almost got knocked over in the hallway. That Miss Alice, she's a mite upset. I held your dinner, didn't think you'd want to invite her."

Maude wiped flour-covered hands on her well-worn cotton apron.

"Come on in the kitchen when you finish your drink."

"Thanks, Maude. You're right. That woman is losing it. I know that she and Ralph have invested a lot of their money in Seaward real estate besides her family's holdings, but she seems to think that her whole life hinges on a bridge from the mainland being built."

"Now you jest tell me what good that would do? All them tourists bring here is dirty laundry and crime in the streets. This is a peaceful place."

"It *was* a peaceful place, anyway, until that boy's murder. Sheriff Hammond is going crazy trying to find out who killed that boy."

"It was them art students," Maude declared, nodding her gray head without a tinge of doubt. "Probably doing awful things: drugs, sex, whatever. You see if that ain't the truth. The little bit of building that's already going on this island has already brought evil. Mark my words. Now, come on and eat your dinner. I fixed some of your favorites: chilled cucumber soup, Aunt Helen's chicken casserole, and for dessert, pecan-brown sugar pound cake."

John glanced at the phone, put his empty glass on the bar, and decided he'd call Maggie tomorrow. After being with his mother all day at the nursing home and dealing with Alice, he'd have dinner, a warm shower, and go to bed early. Maggie was an intriguing person. He'd better go slowly or he'd find himself sinking deeper than a crab in mud. He smiled to himself and called out to Maude, who had returned to the kitchen. "Put the soup on. I'm hungry enough to eat the whole pot."

As John started down the hall, the phone rang. He was tempted to let the machine catch it. Instead, he picked up the receiver.

"Hammond? What's going on? Really? Is Maggie okay? Should I go over there? Thanks. You, too."

John replaced the receiver and walked slowly into the kitchen.

"What's the matter with you?" Maude asked. "You got that look on your face. Musta been Miss Alice jumping on you again."

"No. Sheriff Hammond," John said. He picked up his plate from the pine farm table and started piling chicken casserole on one side.

"Don't you want to eat in the dining room?"

"This is fine. Really, Maude. I'll eat and help you clean the kitchen. I get tired of eating by myself."

"Are you gonna tell what he wants from you? Or is it none of my business?"

"It's Maggie Stewart," John answered.

"Maggie who?"

"Stewart. She's visiting at the Meyers' house. I met her two days ago. She's the one who discovered the murdered boy's body and has had nothing but trouble ever since. Hammond seems to think she's in danger. I can't decide if I should go over there or just call her."

Maude looked at him with alarm. "Don't you do no such thing. I bet you don't even know what kind of folks she comes from."

"Nice ones. Her father was an upcountry judge, I hear, from Rosemont. Relax, Maude. You sound like Mother. I do plan to take her sailing. And maybe see her a few times while she's here. That's all. It's so late, she's probably in bed asleep. I'll call tomorrow."

He smiled broadly at Maude. "That was a great casserole. Wonder if Maggie can cook. You've spoiled me."

John handed his clean plate to Maude and cut himself a large piece of the pound cake.

"If she's a Southern girl," Maude said decisively, "she knows that the way to a man's heart is through his stomach."

"I'll ask her tomorrow. Tonight my stomach's full, and you have once more pleased my heart."

Eight

Maggie finished sun blocking by rubbing a number thirty sun screen onto the cheeks of her oval-shaped face. "I wouldn't be standing here in front of this mirror in the bathroom talking to myself if I had found Possum. I'd be talking to her," Maggie told her reflection. "Yes, yes, I know I said I wouldn't keep her, but damn it, I miss that little puppy." Maggie's lips puckered in the mirror. She picked up the hair brush and began putting her long, blond hair into a beach-style ponytail.

"Not only did I spend most of my morning looking all over this side of Seaward for that dog, I spent the rest of my morning driving around the entire island looking for Dickie Diamond. I can't believe he ran off. It's inconceivable that he tried to attack me. Besides, the man who attacked me lured me to the Liberty Oak. The phone at the Red-Eye doesn't work and, and…"

Maggie popped a rubber band around a clump of her hair and began to tie a lime green ribbon that matched her swim suit around the band. "There. Almost ready for an afternoon of Seaward sun. What a hell of a vacation this is turning into. No dog, no Dickie, and definitely not the jingle of a telephone call from John Heyward. Just who does he think he is anyway? Saying he'll call to invite me sailing, and while I'm being accosted by the man in black, he's playing around with a married woman. But why didn't she spend the night with him, and why, oh why…? Never mind," she told her reflection. "You can't answer the question any better than I can. It's time to quit squandering precious beach time with questions that will never be answered. Even if he called me now, I doubt I would go."

She grabbed her beach bag and headed out the door. There was no sense in locking up now. As Granny Stewart used to say, "It's too late to fasten the gate; the fox is in the hen house."

Small, white, puffy clouds dotted the sky. Early-afternoon sun beamed on the glistening waves. Maggie settled her beach chair into the sand. The beach was almost deserted. Spring was a glorious time for a coastal Carolina vacation.

Down the way, Maggie saw yellow and blue stripes on a canvas beach umbrella. Under the canopy, a lone woman in a bright fuchsia bikini turned the pages of a magazine. It looked like S.J. Styles. In the other direction, a man and woman reclined on loungers near the water's edge. A toddler picked shells from a shallow pool, abandoned by the tide as it rolled back into the ocean. The child brought her shells to the woman. "Sea shell," the child gurgled.

Maggie became engrossed in watching the child. She didn't notice S.J.'s approach until she heard her ask, "May I join you?" S.J. spread her towel next to Maggie's chair without waiting for an answer. "Michael's family has agreed to a memorial service on the island. It's Thursday, three o'clock at the Liberty Oak. You'll come, of course."

A stroke of luck, Maggie thought. She'd be able to see Liberty Oak in daylight and maybe get a fix on the art students. If it was a crime of passion or jealousy, it was likely that one of them would be guilty.

"Yes," Maggie replied. "Are your students able to handle this tragedy?"

"Well, of course, none of them knew him well, but everyone was shocked, and it's always hard to accept the death of one so young, especially when he died in such a violent way. The students will be going home after the service. We'll have a two-week break, then do the art show. The sheriff has confirmed their alibis, by the way, not that any of them were suspects.

"Michael was chosen the Findley Scholar for the Carter Institute. I don't think he would have wanted to spend the summer here. Now we'll never know. I still can't believe it happened. Senseless. I hope you've been able to enjoy our island this week, in spite of everything. Where is the cute puppy that you found? She'd love running on the beach."

"I've lost her," Maggie said. "She ran away last night. I hope she'll turn up. I've spent a considerable amount of time and money on her. I named her Possum. I have no idea whose dog she was. Maybe she came on the island with a family on a day trip and got left behind. If you hear anything, let me know."

Maggie heard a strange beep. "What's that?" she asked.

"My sun-watch. It's a device that measures the sun's UVB rays. It tells me when I've had enough." S.J. stuck her arm out, and Maggie looked at the watch. S.J. pointed to the dial. "You enter your skin type and the SPF of your sunscreen. This display shows how much exposure you've had, how strong the sun is, and when it's time for you to go in the shade. Clever, isn't it? Although it doesn't always work properly. Sometimes, it just starts beeping."

Maggie nodded, pretending that she hadn't lost interest.

"Time for me to get myself off the beach. Did Hammond come by your house last night? I saw a truck in the driveway."

"I had a break-in last night. Nothing taken. Just a mess."

"This is horrible. Our island is turning into a major crime area. I'm so sorry. I hope they find the culprit."

Maggie dropped the conversation. The poor woman had enough to think about without listening to her problems. And Maggie had never been one for gossip. She didn't want her experiences discussed all over the island.

"Deputy Watson's exact words to me were, 'Don't worry your pretty little head.' He's a jerk."

S.J. laughed. "But he's right, you know. Michael's dead. We must get on with our lives. It's hurting the reputation of our art internships. Headlines every day in the *Mainland Gazette*." S.J. paused for breath and dusted the sand off her legs. The sand blew into Maggie's face.

"Are any of your students into drugs?" Maggie asked.

"Drugs? No way. Most of them don't even drink. Absurd. Does the sheriff think that?"

"The sheriff and his deputy don't seem to be thinking at all."

"There's my second beep. Out of the sun for me. See you at the service at Liberty Oak. Enjoy your vacation." S.J. trotted down the beach.

The warm rays of the spring sun lulled Maggie into a peaceful half-doze. She wanted to push thoughts of John from her mind, but she couldn't. There was something about him that drew her. She breathed a deep sigh and let the thoughts come. Her response to his kiss had been natural. But Alice had been with him last night. He had mentioned sailing. He hadn't called. Maybe she should declare this trip a disaster and go home. There wouldn't be any need for a call. She'd be two hundred miles away. Why didn't he call? Alice, she thought. The question was answered.

"Soaking up the rays?" Maggie's eyes flew open. She stared straight into Dickie Diamond's gap-toothed grin.

"Why did you leave me last night? Where in hell have you been? Why did you run?"

"Hammond found me. Why'd you tell him I was with you? Now Sally Jo's gonna find out. I walked from here all the way to Sally Jo's trailer. Told her my truck broke down at Liberty Oak. If Sally Jo found out I was with you, there would be hell to pay. She'd scratch your eyes out. I done told you how jealous she is. And then she'd kill me and stuff my body in the crab processing machine. She done told me that a gazillion times. And the damn sheriff's threatening to pull my liquor license again. Thought I was selling beer at Liberty Oak last night. Since I was with you, he can't blame me for the break-in. I'm sorry about that. But Sally Jo—she's a real jealous woman."

"Maybe she has reason to be. After all, you came on to me the first time I met you," Maggie reminded him.

Dickie rubbed the toe of his tennis shoe in the sand. He wouldn't look directly at Maggie.

"Dickie, I'm going to forgive you for running away last night if you'll please get the locks changed on my doors. Somebody must have made a copy of that key I lost. He's coming in and out like he's in a revolving door."

"I already decided to do that. I called Malcolm's Hardware from your phone. Said he'd send over dead bolt locks on the *Mary Grace* this afternoon. I'll pick 'em up with my deliveries."

"How could you use my phone? Oh, wait. I guess I didn't lock the doors."

"The front door was wide open when I drove up. I walked in and called for you. Oh, I almost forgot. The phone was ringing. Mister Heyward wants you to call him back. Left his number. Said he'd been over on the mainland all morning. Reckon Alice went to see him soon as she got home. She's a piece of work. Anyways, he's giving you an invite to sail tomorrow."

By this time, Maggie and Dickie had reached the front door of the beach house. "Let me go in and make sure it's okay," Dickie said.

Maggie nodded. "I'll wait here for you, but be careful. I know that even if I didn't lock the doors, I did leave them closed."

Dickie disappeared through the door, stomping his feet and making loud noises. Maggie wondered if she should really return John's call. A day of sailing would be fun, but that's all it would be, she reminded herself.

75

"All clear," Dickie called. "Come on in. Doesn't look like any-body's been here. Sure you closed this door tight before you went to the beach?"

"I thought I did."

Dickie walked down the steps and started toward his truck. "I'll get your locks this afternoon. Don't worry. By the way, the sheriff also told me that the ribbon you found at Liberty Oak wasn't the same kind of ribbon as you found at the murder scene."

"What?"

"I'd be kinda nervous if I was you. You being in the wrong places at the wrong times."

"Nonsense. And if you don't fix my locks, I'll tell Sally Jo that you've been hanging around with me."

A look of terror swept over Dickie's face. "You wouldn't do that, now would you, Miss Maggie?"

"Just go get the locks, put them in, and give me, and only me, the keys."

Maggie walked into the house. A rustling noise came from the back bedroom. "Dickie!" she hollered. "Come back." She heard the sound of his truck going down the road. The rustling grew louder and then became a gnawing sound.

Maggie stood frozen on the spot, not sure what to do. Then she saw a furry little head peek around the door.

"Oh, my God!" she cried. She wasn't sure if it was a cry of joy, re-lief, or horror. "Possum!" The dog was carrying a half-chewed shoe, half of the only pair of Ferragamo shoes that Maggie had brought with her.

"Oh, Possum, you're back!" Maggie scooped the dog into her lap and hugged and kissed her soft puppy fur. Possum licked her face and swiped Maggie's hair with a joyfully wagging tail.

"But look what you've done! My best shoes, my favorite dressy shoes. Listen, muttsy, when we get back to Rosemont, you're going to obedience school. Now that I've officially adopted you, let's feed, water, and kennel you. You can teethe on the plastic toys I bought you."

By the time Maggie took care of Possum, finished her shower, and put on a favorite white cotton nightie, the sun was beginning to set. At last, she felt comfortable enough to return John's call. She'd thought through several approaches and decided to be straightforward. Accept the invitation, say thank you, and see you tomorrow. That would suffice. John answered on the third ring. Not enough time for Maggie to change her mind again and hang up.

"I was getting ready to call you again," John said. "Are you okay?"

The tone of his voice punched a button inside Maggie, and before she could control her thoughts or words, she told him about her day.

"I want you to get those locks changed. If Dickie hasn't done it by the time we're back from sailing, then I'll do it myself. We are going sailing tomorrow, aren't we? The weather's supposed to be perfect. I have a surprise destination for you. No, I'm going to wait until tomorrow and show you. Are you okay, Maggie?"

The sob wouldn't stay in her throat. "I'm just exhausted from threats, break-ins, and all the horrors that have occurred since I've been on the island," she cried.

"Stay where you are. I'll be over in less than fifteen minutes."

John arrived in less time than that. Maggie was sitting on the deck counting stars and trying to keep her mind numb until he got there.

She stood up and moved toward him, forgetting that she'd planned to put on her denim jumpsuit before he arrived.

He walked over to her and put his arms around her slender waist. She felt his tongue on her lips. She opened her mouth and embraced him with her nightie-clad body.

77

Nine

Maggie cupped her hand across her forehead to escape the bright sun. A perfect sailing day. Fair weather and a breeze. None of the boats moored at Markley's Landing looked familiar. The mystery boat wasn't here. But John's sloop was in slot ten. Maggie waved to him and walked down the dock to his slip. "Permission to come aboard, sir?"

A broad grin twinkled across his face as Maggie stepped aboard. "Permission granted," he said as he hugged her.

It was a casual, glad-to-see-you hug, but Maggie could feel strong emotion behind it. That hadn't been there before last night. Even sitting next to him in her nightie had not been awkward. They spent hours discussing the murder. His concern for her safety from the man in black was evident. He held her hand and rubbed the back of her neck while they talked. She wondered if they would have kept talking until the wee hours of the morning or if... But she fell asleep with her head in his lap.

This morning, Possum jumped on her at seven. When she staggered out to tend to the dog, John was still in his clothes, sprawled on his back across the guest room bed, snoring lightly through his open mouth. Wow, Maggie thought, he's handsome even when he snores. And he was even better looking now, in the sunshine, with that gorgeous twinkle in his deep-blue eyes. Maggie shook her silky blond hair and pulled her thoughts back to the present.

"This isn't what I imagined," she said. "You said a small sailboat. This has a mast and two sails."

"It's twenty-three feet. My regatta boat. I just got a weather update. We're leaving this baby home today. Come on. We're going to Port Royale for lunch on the *Sea Song*. She has an inboard motor.

If we keep an eye on the weather, we can outrun a storm with her powerful engine."

"But it's a gorgeous day. There are just a few wispy clouds in the sky."

"Cirrus. It's a 'mackerel sky.' The weather's changing, could be for the worse. Port Royale's down the inland waterway. Easier to get back if the weather changes. Besides, we'll have time to talk." He placed his arm around her waist and smiled.

Maggie and John settled on board the *Sea Song*.

"This is bigger than your sailboat. You're a real salt," Maggie said.

"Well, remember, this island has always been my home. Mother wants to come home. She's worse. I've been with her on the mainland most days this month." John started the engine and headed toward the waterway.

Waves sloshed against the boat. Small whitecaps hit the bow as the shoreline disappeared. Maggie felt the salty spray on her face.

"A lot's happened since I've been here," she said. "This isn't the kind of vacation I needed. It's frightening. Dickie's changing the locks and baby sitting for Possum today. I'm glad we're getting away."

"I was talking to Hammond this morning. He thinks you know more than you're telling him. He's thinking of questioning you again."

"You told him you'd talk to me today?"

"No, I didn't We don't have to discuss this; only if it makes you feel better. I think we covered it all last night."

"I...I saw Alice coming like a bat out of hell from your house. Want to discuss that?" Maggie rubbed the temples on her head.

John ignored the question. "Relax. Have a headache?" He reached over and began to rub the back of her neck.

Maggie smelled his delicious after-shave pleasantly mingling with salty air.

"Look! A porpoise leaping up in the water. A whole school, off the left of the bow," Maggie said, as she strained to get a closer look.

John shut the engine down and watched the gray, long-nosed mammals coming closer to the boat with each dive they took. "They rarely come this close. They're looking for food: crustaceans and other small fish."

"Tell me more," Maggie said.

"When you live around the ocean, and want to protect it, you learn about its environment. The name porpoise is from the old French word for hog-fish. Ugly name for a beautiful creature. There's one jumping beside the boat. Hey, Flipper."

"I want to touch it," Maggie said, as she leaned over the side of the boat. She felt John's arms close around her.

"Don't fall in," he said. The porpoise swam away.

Maggie turned from the gurgling water and leaned into his body. She felt his response. The attraction was powerful, but something made her hesitate. Did she truly trust him? Finally, she gently pushed him away and said in a loud voice, "Where'd you say we're having lunch?"

"Port Royale. We're almost there." John turned from Maggie and started the engine. She saw disappointment on his face.

"Our Port Royale's a sea island," he said, "inhabited originally by copper-skinned natives. Frenchman Jean Ribaut brought a group of French Huguenots over around 1562. They were probably the first settlers. More recent settlers carry clubs and collect alligators on their shirt pockets. Their tribal ritual seems to be running up and down greens, yelling 'fore' while they swing these clubs."

Maggie laughed. In the distance, a shoreline with wide, even beaches appeared. "There are times when I want to chuck it all. Quit fighting the damn tourists and sail away. I can't halt develop-

81

ment on these sea islands forever. Hopefully, I can contain some of the fallout. At least my attorneys are working on a deal to make part of my holdings on Seaward a National Wildlife Preserve."

John eased the *Sea Song* into the Port Royale Harbour. Maggie had her first glimpse of the tiny sea island.

The island was laden with large, tall pines and huge, old palmetto trees, some casting their skinny shadows across the white, sandy beach. The marshy land behind the beach was overgrown with sea oats. John and Maggie walked through a wooded clearing and stepped into the opening of a crepe myrtle-banked garden. Behind the garden, a two-story pillared mansion depicted the Carolina Lowcountry mystique. A piazza on the front loomed above.

"A real plantation," Maggie exclaimed.

"The Elliot Inn," John said. "Been here forever. Not many tourists make it out to this part of Port Royale. Piker and his daughter, Karisima, have been dishing up meals for a select few for years. If you call ahead, they'll have lunch ready for you. Let's see what's on the menu today."

The sounds of harp, flute, and clarinet wafted out the door as they entered the long entrance hall. Jasmine-scented air mingled with the scents of Southern fried cooking. Silver crystal and white linen graced the banquet table in the dining room.

"Piker, this is my friend, Maggie Stewart. Maggie, Piker's tales of chasing giant devil fish are the best stories ever told, aren't they, Piker?"

Piker chuckled and led them down the hall, out the door, and into a profusion of flowers in the garden. A table for two was set in the white gazebo in the middle of the garden. A view of the beach and ocean beyond formed the backdrop for their lunch.

"Today Karisima's gonna give you Saint Cecilia's Punch and shrimp remoulade with crackers while you enjoy the view. I'll be back in two shakes of a cow's tail."

82

Maggie breathed deeply and looked into John's bright blue eyes. They sat across from each other in comfortable silence. Piker came back and placed the appetizers and drinks in front of them. Maggie took her first sip.

"Tastes a little like Long Island Ice Tea," she said.

"Rum, peach brandy, champagne, tea, and Karisima's secret ingredients," John said. "She and my cook, Maude, are the best this side of heaven. Karisima and Piker's family have worked for the Elliots, who own this place, for generations. She and Piker helped open it as an inn about five years ago. They cater to honeymoon couples from other parts of the world. Only take six or eight guests at a time."

"Thanks for sharing this wonderful place with me," Maggie said. She reached across the table and entwined her fingers with his. He placed a cracker with shrimp remoulade to her lips. "Yum," she said.

"There are plenty of stories about our barrier islands. After Confederate President Jefferson Davis was captured, the prison ship taking him to Fortress Monroe in Virginia stopped here, probably right there on the beach in front of us. Piker's great-grandfather claimed he saw him. Our islands are full of oral history, passed on to new generations."

"What will future generations say about the murder of Michael McKay?" Maggie asked him.

"It's tragic. If Hammond ties this up quickly, it'll be forgotten. Maybe it'll keep the tourists away for a while."

"That's a lousy motive for a murder," Maggie said.

Piker set steaming bowls of Carolina she-crab soup on the table and eased away. Maggie and John continued to enjoy the view, each other, and the food.

"Hammond doesn't seem to have found a motive yet," Maggie said. "He's sending the art students home. Says they all had air-tight alibis. I've already told you that three times, haven't I? That doesn't leave many suspects. Hammond even had the audacity to tell me Toot Sweet was harmless."

She couldn't leave it. The murder was haunting her mind. "Tell me about Toot Sweet."

"Well," John said, "his real name is Leroy Sweet, Jr. Leroy Senior has been in the penitentiary for most of Toot's life. Toot's mama's a little batty. She kept trying to find a way to bake a cake with a saw inside it, so Leroy Senior could bust out of jail."

"So, do you think Toot is harmless?"

"Everybody on Seaward is, or I thought they were. I've known most of those people all of my life. Since Ralph and Alice started their development of Seaward, there have been some newcomers, but they are few and well fixed for money."

"How can you be so close to Alice? She and Ralph are desecrating your island. Soon you'll have a bridge, traffic lights, and Rodeo Drive-type boutiques."

"Leave Alice out of this," John said, suddenly testy. "She's doing what she has to do. You don't know her."

"How can you defend such a..." Maggie was interrupted in mid-sentence by their main course.

"The soup was excellent," John said to Piker. "What's next?"

"Karisima went all out today," Piker answered. "Tomato-okra pilau, corn sticks, roasted wild duck with orange stuffing, and her famous chainey briar."

"What's that?" Maggie asked.

"Wild asparagus in some concoction of hers. Best eating you ever had. When you done, Karisima says she has a couple slices of Huguenot torte left over from last night. Enjoy." Piker lifted the cover from the silver serving dish and withdrew toward the kitchen. John began filling their plates.

"I could stay here and eat forever," Maggie said.

"Me, too. After lunch we'll meet Karisima and take a quick tour of the island before we return to Seaward."

"Capital idea." Maggie tasted her first bit of chainey briar. "This is to die for. Sorry. Just an expression. But, John, I'm not going to let this push me back to Rosemont. I've been trying to make life-altering decisions for months. I needed to be totally away. I haven't been able to keep the murder out of my thoughts, but I need to be thinking of major decisions. Do I even want to continue designing other people's interiors? I want to do my own. I have ideas that could create my dream residence, but..."

"The way your eyes light up when you say that, you've too much energy to let it go down the drain. Maybe a vacation will help you, or a change to new clients and their new attitudes. From what you've told me, the people in Rosemont want to have the same things but more of them. You need clients that present a challenge. Who cares what color the rugs are in your clients' houses in Rosemont? A bunch of biddies who want the same color, style, make, and model. You need relocation to fulfill your dreams."

Maggie laughed. "I suppose you're right. I'll think about it. The duck is delicious. I won't need to eat for the rest of the week. I'll just jog twice a day."

John put down his fork and looked at the sky. "We need to be going soon. Let's get Piker to give us a quick tour and save the dessert for another day."

"Great with me."

Maggie and John met Piker at the door. "I was just a-coming to check on you. What's wrong? You ain't ordered your Huguenot torte."

"Wrap it to go," John said. "I can smell a storm coming by the waterway. Can't you? I did want Maggie to have a quick tour of the house."

"Yeah, afternoon shower probably heading this way. But you ain't getting a quick tour. Miz Elliot is in residence and just biding her time until your lunch was over. Oh boy, here she comes. I hear her a-tapping on the stairs."

A regal-looking, silver-haired woman, dressed in elegant blue silk and leaning on a cane, came into the room. "John, what would your mother say if she knew you'd brought a beautiful lady to lunch at my house and didn't perform the gentlemanly duties of introducing us?"

Ten

The inn was decorated in a beautiful array of colors, and yet it remained true to its historical significance and offered comfort for its guests.

"Colors have language. I like the ones that speak to my heart," Maggie commented.

The Elliot house had been magnificent. She and John walked hand-in-hand down the dock and jumped aboard the *Sea Song*. Black clouds swirled on the horizon.

"Karisima was not what I expected," Maggie said. "I heard her father mention she had trained at Johnson-Wales. That's a world-renowned chef institute. Piker said they are descendants of slaves. He's traced their ancestors back to the auction blocks of Savannah. When my mother used to laugh about Southerners being like the Chinese—eating rice and worshiping their ancestors—I didn't understand. It's important to know your family, isn't it?"

John pushed the *Sea Song* away from the dock, smiling at Maggie and nodding his head. The wind had come up, and it was getting harder for them to talk to each other. She walked over and put her arms around him. "Thank you," she said. "That was a great day."

"It's a lovely secret hideaway," he answered.

As John powered the boat along the waterway, Maggie stretched her legs across the back of the boat and closed her eyes. Was she ready to finish that kiss? Would it bring a beginning? She sighed and let her mind drift with the drone of the boat engine. Would Hammond solve the murder, and would she start a relationship with John? She had more questions than answers, as always. If Dickie had changed the locks as promised, maybe she'd have no more trouble. Hammond could figure out why someone wanted to frighten her and try to prevent her from being involved. The few loose pieces of the puzzle could go unsolved. Toot Sweet and Joe, the security guard, could continue to make deliveries—drugs, probably—long after the murder was solved. But why hadn't she seen Joe at the gate for the last two days? She'd have to check on that. A sudden squeal jarred her thoughts. John was tuning the Coast Guard radio.

"What's wrong?" she asked.

"Look at the sky," John said.

Maggie felt a stiff breeze on her face. The darkening sky announced the presence of a storm. The appearance of a thunderhead above the horizon confirmed the storm was near. Maggie felt chilled. The temperature had dropped. Sudden gusts of cold wind struck the boat savagely. Maggie reached for John's arm. He grabbed her and pulled her to him.

"It'll be short duration. More like a summer burst. That's a cumulus-nimbus cloud. Dirty bottom with an anvil top, white caps, rain underneath. Go below. We'll be safe. I'm heading for Tom Murphy's dock. Just a mile or two up the way."

"I'm not going to be stuck below without you if we capsize," Maggie screamed over the wind.

The rain began to beat on her face. John kept steering and looked straight ahead. "We're too big to capsize. I'm worried about lightning striking the boat. Okay, stay here next to me."

Maggie felt the churning of the ocean beneath the boat. Waves hit the sides and rocked her against John. He smiled and patted her shoulder. "I've been through lots of these," he said. "The life jackets are in the locker underneath that bench. Want to get them for me?"

"Life jackets? You're serious?"

Thunder crashed against Maggie's ears. Lightning bolts danced across the dark sky. John held her closer and managed to steer the boat with one hand. Maggie closed her eyes. She didn't want to see. She opened her eyes. She didn't want to die with her eyes closed.

"Look, Maggie, the Murphys' dock. We're there. We'll be warm and dry soon."

Maggie breathed a sigh of relief. The *Sea Song,* sturdy and proud, swayed alongside the dock. John cut the engine. "Grab the line by the bow," he told her. "Use a figure eight and fasten it to the cleat on the dock."

A bolt of lightning hit a tree on the bank near the dock. The crash jolted the foundation of the weathered boards. Maggie dropped the rope and ran for her life. The door to the cottage opened. A warm glow cast its shadow across the porch.

Maggie jumped across the threshold, skidded onto a hard, wooden floor, and landed on her backside. Water dripped off her shaking body.

"John. John? Are you coming?" Maggie, on all fours, peered out the door.

Tom Murphy walked across the porch to greet John. "What's the cat drug in this time? You come to pay your poker debts?"

"My crew jumped ship," John said with a laugh. "Took a while to tie her down by myself. We're looking for a haven in the storm. Maggie, meet my friend and cousin, Tom."

Maggie rose from the floor and shook hands. "Sorry. I didn't mean to be rude. I've never been in a storm like this."

"You shoulda seen Hugo. Now that was a mighty force. Lost part of our roof. We were luckier than most. Come on in. Down this hall. My wife, Julie, and the kids are riding it out playing charades. Julie insists we unplug the TV during storms."

Maggie and John followed Tom toward the noisy chatter of children, playing games on a rainy day. "Here's a towel and some dry clothes, Maggie. Step in this bedroom and change. You'll be more comfortable." Tom handed Maggie a small pile of neatly folded shorts and shirts. "Something ought to fit you. Don't know what I got for you, John. You gained weight? Going out with Alice every night while Ralph was in Europe put some pounds on you."

The two men walked on down the hall.

Maggie stepped into the bedroom and closed the door. She didn't want to hear about Alice. Rain beat fiercely against the window panes. Howling wind drowned out the sounds of the children down the hall.

John's friends knew about Alice. The time had come for a serious talk. She couldn't let herself get caught up in another relationship that was doomed from the start. If the storm lasted long enough, an opportunity to talk to Julie would arise. The Murphys seemed to be John's longtime friends and family.

A blue and white striped shirt and white denim shorts hugged Maggie's body. At least she was dry and clean. She ran her fingers through her hair and stepped over to the mirror above a tall oak dresser. Then she saw it: red ribbon. It was shorter than the ribbon she had seen at Liberty Oak. A child's hair ribbon? Or another one the killer planned to use? She left the ribbon on the dresser just as she had found it.

Chaos reigned in the den. John was swinging a small boy around the room. The kids screamed in delight. Two little girls jumped up and down hollering, "I wanna be next."

Blond and quiet, Julie Murphy worked embroidery thread through her needlepoint canvas. Her needle moved smoothly and rhythmically with each stitch. She looked up and smiled as Maggie entered the room.

"This is Maggie," John shouted above the confusion. "Maggie, meet my cousin, Julie."

"Are all three yours?" Maggie asked, as she stepped over blocks and crayons. She settled on the sofa next to Julie.

"Yes. It's been a trying week. I didn't expect to spend our entire spring vacation inside the house."

"Uncle John's got a girlfriend." The children were shouting and jumping up and down on the furniture. "John and Maggie sitting in a tree, K-I-S-S-I-N-G."

"John and I just met this week," Maggie said to Julie. She hesitated for a moment, but knew she had to ask about Alice. She had always been impulsive. Now was not the time for a personality make-over. "I suppose he's been friends with Alice for a long time."

"They're friends, that's all, at least from John's point of view." Julie answered without dropping a stitch of her needlepoint pillow. "About a year ago, he was engaged to Laura Summers. She was transferred to Colorado, worked for a computer company. John wanted to stay here. He broke the engagement. If you really want my opinion, I don't think he loved her.

"He doesn't love Alice either, if you want to know the truth. But she and Ralph have separated. Happened this morning. John told Tom this morning on the phone. I guess I shouldn't be gossiping like this, but I hope you see more of John. He's such a wonderful person."

Maggie realized she needed to put this information in the back of her head and think about it later. If John knew Alice was separated and still chose to spend such a wonderful day with her, then...

"See the picture I just colored?" A blond, pale, skinny child stopped singing and walked over to Maggie. Red blotches covered her arms and legs.

Maggie accepted the scribbled paper from the child, hugged her tightly, kissed her cheek and said, "Too much sun this week. I bet it'll turn brown soon."

"Naw, we been in the house all week," the little girl replied. "It's chicken pox. Only I didn't get it from chickens. My sister Mandy gave it to me."

"Chicken pox!" Maggie cried. She recoiled instantly from the small child. "I've never had chicken pox."

91

Eleven

"Morning," Hammond said. "Come on in."

John closed the door to the cramped space that Sheriff Hammond called an office. It was the only available space on the island, and the marina, part of which Hammond had turned into an office, was centrally located. But Markley Marina needed a major renovation. It had been standing in its present spot since the 1950s. The owners, a family from upstate Maine, came down once a year and stayed at the Seaward Inn. They refused to even patch the leaks in the roof. If the island ever started booming, they declared, Markley Marina would be a major priority on their list. That was fine. Years ago, the owners put the marina on a real estate market listing, and rumor had it they spent their vacations on Aruba. Hammond had commandeered the inner office of the cement block building, rent free, to use when he wasn't at the county offices on the mainland. No one cared. Spider Jones sold fish bait, gassed up the few boats that came by, and met the *Mary Grace* when she brought mainlanders over.

After dusting off the wooden ladder-back chair in front of the desk, John sat down. He'd donned a pair of khakis and a white shirt this morning with the intention of going to the memorial service for the boy who had been murdered, if Maggie continued to insist that they should go.

"What's up?" he said to Hammond. "I got your message. I suppose you want to know if I talked to Maggie about the murder. She doesn't know anything. Someone may think she does. It'd be better if you left her alone and concentrated on another angle."

"What other angle?" Hammond asked. "Watson and I have followed up on every lead. There aren't many. It was a crime of passion from the looks of that boy's bashed-in skull. Most all of these

93

islanders are too damn lazy to work up that much steam. That poor kid was mutilated. We were lucky to be able to make an identification. The coroner's report hasn't helped much either. But you don't want to hear about my problems. I think you've got enough of your own. I see Alice heading this way. Bet she's looking for you."

John glanced out the grimy plate glass window and frowned. "She and Ralph are having a few problems right now. Because of the closeness of our families, she considers me a friend."

"I'll just bet she does," Hammond said, grinning, and then his face grew serious again. "The murderer is probably in Rio by now. This case will go down unsolved."

"Bad publicity for Seaward Island, but leave Maggie out of it. She's here for a quiet vacation and doesn't want or need to be involved with complications to put her in a dangerous situation."

"Did she say to tell me that?" the sheriff asked, sounding annoyed.

"No, I'm telling you. She's not involved in any way."

"Oh, but I think she is. Finding the body put her right smack-dab in the middle of it. I won't do anything to endanger her, but if she encounters one more threat then I'm gonna have to take drastic measures, maybe have Watson guard her until she decides to go home. His idea, not mine. He thinks she's kinda cute."

"Well, I don't think she feels the same way. You keep that S.O.B. out of her way."

Hammond laughed out loud. "Touchy, aren't we? Oh, no. Here's Alice. It'll be interesting to see how you handle this."

"Damn it, Hammond. If I hadn't known you all my life, I think I'd haul off and... Good morning, Alice. Looking for Hammond? He's holding court in his Seaward office this morning."

"John, darling. You've got to take me to the memorial service. S.J. expects me to be there. I cannot bear to go alone. Be a dear and say yes. Oh, hello, Sheriff. Caught any crooks lately?"

"I'll be done here in a few minutes," John told her. "Then we'll talk about the service. Wait for me outside, please."

"I'm not going to take no for an answer," Alice said, giving John a determined smile. "But I will wait outside. It smells to high heaven in here. Spider's fish bait seems to be riper than usual."

Alice flounced toward the door and ignored Spider as she held her nose and walked out, banging the screen door as she went.

"Now, she's a real handful, ain't she?" Hammond commented.

John went back to the matter he had come to discuss. "Seriously, don't put Maggie into a dangerous position. If you want to flush out the killer, find another way to do it."

"Sounds like you're interested in this woman. Seen a lot of her since she's been here?"

"Not enough. I'm going to use your phone to let her know I'll just meet her at the service. Wouldn't be wise to pick her up with Alice in the car."

"I think not. Now that she and Ralph have separated, you're gonna have your hands plum full. Not sure I'd want to be in your shoes. Be careful. Ralph has a temper. Wouldn't want him naming you in some sort of sex scandal," Hammond said, and he threw his head back and guffawed.

"Not a chance. Got a phone book in this shack? One that hasn't been chewed on by your deputized mice?"

"Think I'll go pump Alice for any new island gossip while you whisper sweet nothings into that pretty little lady's ear. Here's you a phone book."

John picked up the receiver and dialed Maggie's number.

Twelve

Three hours later, the islanders congregated to pay their last respects to a boy who had never lived there. Bodies swayed to and fro in a wide circle. The entire group joined in singing "Amazing Grace". Maggie clutched the pearls around her neck as if the necklace were a rosary. Coming to Michael's memorial service may have been a mistake. John, leaning into the beat of the gospel song, seemed restless, too. Maggie's eyes wandered around the circle of people. One of these islanders was her attacker, maybe even the killer. The music ceased after the third chorus, and a student who had known Michael before he came to the island stepped forward to say a few words.

S.J. stood in the background dabbing her eyes.

Maggie's thoughts wandered to another new worry. She thought about yesterday's visit to Doctor Reid, a psychiatrist renting the cottage around the corner from Maggie. He diagnosed the chicken pox problem with a hearty laugh. "Fourteen to twenty-one days," he told her, "and then you'll either have 'em or you won't. Adults get shingles." He went into gory details of what seemed to Maggie a dreaded, painful disease.

"What does a shrink know about childhood diseases?" she asked herself, hoping mightily that he was wrong. She'd gone to see him because he was the only doctor on Seaward.

In twenty-one days, Maggie would be standing in a client's freshly painted dining room, trying to convince her that just because the Alexanders had put their corner cupboard in the living room, it wasn't necessary for her to do the same. She would tell the client that her cupboard, a classic with strong, simple lines, looked perfect just where it was. Then Maggie would jump up and down screaming in agony from little red bumps that were popping out all

97

over her body, and the client would fire her immediately, not because of the chicken pox, but because she'd undoubtedly think Maggie was throwing a fit to get her way. She almost laughed out loud but remembered in time that she was at a memorial service. Maggie shook the image from her head.

A slight sea breeze wafted across the crowd. It caught the red ribbon sashes the art students had tied around their waists. Red ribbons fluttered through the circle. Maggie remembered the blood around Michael's head in the lagoon. The students chose to display their sympathies in very poor taste, she thought.

John touched her arm. "It'll be over soon," he whispered.

Sheriff Hammond and Deputy Watson stood on the opposite side of the memorial circle. A familiar face stood next to the sheriff. Maggie knew she'd seen him somewhere, perhaps on the mainland in a crowd of tourists. He could have been on the *Mary Grace*, one of the commuters. His height and weight were the same build as her attacker. Maggie shook her head. She needed to be closer to this man, find out where she'd met him.

"Wonderful service, wasn't it?" Alice said when the service concluded and people began to drift away. "I want all my friends to say nice things about me after I'm gone."

"What friends?" Maggie thought. Alice was holding John's arm and smiling. Maggie looked across the crowd and began to inch her way toward the sheriff. By the time she moved next to him, the man in the white poplin pants had disappeared. The crowd was thinning. Dickie Diamond was walking toward his truck with Sally Jo. He had given Maggie the high sign, but hadn't introduced Sally Jo.

The three musicians were packing their instruments. "Come hear us tonight at the Red-Eye," one said. "We're playing 'til one a.m."

"Who was the man standing next to you during the service?" Maggie asked the sheriff.

"New renter on the island," he said, "retired from some Northern company. Thinking about settling here. Think his name is Robert Davis. Ask S.J. He seems to be with her all the time. He walked up the beach. Musta parked his car up there."

"Yes. That's where I saw him, at S.J.'s party. He was getting a drink at the bar. He's the perfect build for my attacker and looks like one of the men I saw in the boat. He knew Michael if he knows S.J. I've got to find him."

"Whoa, little lady, you got no proof. I'll check into it. Let's get all this into its proper perspective. First, you stole the red ribbon from the murder scene. You say that your house was broken into with a key you lost, and yet nothing was taken. You've been threatened on the mainland, and chased around the Liberty Oak."

Hammond paused for a breath, a wide grin spreading across his face. He tried to cover it with his hand. "And yesterday, I heard you were attacked by the chicken pox."

Maggie turned away. For the rest of her vacation, not only would she avoid Hammond, but would seriously take matters into her own hands. Dickie could certainly help her.

John and Alice walked over to Maggie. "I haven't seen you this upset since yesterday at Tom and Julie's," John said, putting his hand on her shoulder. "Was the service too unorthodox for you?"

"It's Sheriff Hammond," Maggie retorted. "He's driving me nuts. I've never dealt with anyone like him. Walk up the beach with me. I'm looking for Robert Davis. John, that man is shaped just like my assailant. He's a friend of S.J.'s. He knew Michael. I want to talk with him."

"Robert? You think Robert had something to do with Michael's murder? Maggie, Robert's a respectable businessman. Retired. He's taken S.J. out a few times. That's his only crime. How anyone can be around her for more than ten minutes, I'll never know," John said.

"John, darling, you're talking about one of my nearest and dearest friends," Alice said.

Maggie turned and walked up the beach. "Coming?"

John and Alice caught up with her. Alice had her slingback heels in her hand. "Maggie, dear, what makes you think you can solve a crime that even our sheriff hasn't been able to do?" Alice asked.

"Simple," Maggie said. "Follow the premise that the truth can be known and acted upon. Motive, psychological make-up, opportunity, and means. The investigation expands until you've narrowed it down. Hammond doesn't have a logical thought in his brain."

"My, what a silly notion you have. Hammond would be intrigued," Alice said.

"If he understood at all," John added.

"Thanks, John. Will you help?"

"Be careful, Maggie, these threats are real. Did Dickie get your locks changed?"

"Not yet. He promised to try again this afternoon. I guess he's over there now."

"No, he had to get back to the Red-Eye. Said he left Toot tending the bar. That character will drink him out of business if he's gone too long," John said.

"I still don't trust Toot," Maggie said. "I wish I knew more about him."

"Tom Murphy told me this story yesterday. Toot's always wanted to learn to drive, begged people to teach him. He used to work for Tom. After Toot dropped out of high school, Tom got him this job at Larry's Island Garage. When Larry's old man died, the family let Toot work on Clyde's car: the old, green, rusted-out Cadillac, an antique really. Told him if he could make it run they wouldn't charge him for the parts. It was the happiest day of Toot's life. He fixed the car, but couldn't drive it. Since then, Clyde gave him the car and taught him to drive."

"Toot Sweet knows Tom Murphy? Does he still work for him?" Maggie asked.

"I think he still does yard work for him. Why?"

"Nothing. I could just be seeing red. I'll bet Toot has been at the Murphys' recently. Will you check for me, John? I'll also wager that Toot is connected to Robert Davis. Probably works for him, too."

"I don't see Robert anywhere," Alice said. "We've walked at least a half mile from Liberty Oak. He couldn't possibly be your attacker. He's such an adorable man. Remember, John, he and S.J. played tennis with us last week? Besides, Maggie, what would you say if you found him? 'Excuse me, Robert, but did you kill Michael and attack me to shut me up?' Really, Maggie, you're too much."

Maggie bit her tongue. If she told Alice to drop dead, John would probably be upset. Better to just ignore the bitch. That, of course, was not possible.

"John, be a dear and go get the car," Alice said. "I cannot sludge back in this sand. The tide's coming in. Maggie and I'll wait here for you."

"Sorry, Alice," Maggie said. "I'm walking back to my car with John. See you later."

"I know you don't like Alice," John said when they were out of earshot. "Give her a chance. She's having a hard time. She needs me. We've been friends forever."

"If we plan to continue to see each other, let's not include Alice, okay?"

"Fine. I'll take Alice home and give you a call. We'll go to dinner tonight."

"Sounds great. I'm going home now," Maggie called over her shoulder to John. She walked toward the Volvo.

Neither of them saw the black-clad figure hidden behind the tree a few yards from their cars. The figure stood silently, watching Maggie as she drove away.

101

Thirteen

The portable phone rested on the deck table beside Maggie. Possum curled up in her lap.

Happy that she was home, Maggie stretched her legs and took a sip of sweet iced tea. The late afternoon sun felt warm but not stifling. It had been at least an hour since she'd been back, and John hadn't called. Alice was probably being difficult, maybe trying to get John to take her out for dinner. Dickie had not changed the locks, nor had he even been over today. He was as slow and irresponsible as a shell washed in by the tide.

"Bet ya been looking for me," Dickie said as he walked up the deck steps. "After the service, I had to take Sally Jo to her mother's trailer. Gawd, them women."

"I hope you're here to change my locks. I'll feel safer. I have decided that in spite of what everyone thinks, Toot is involved in Michael's murder."

Dickie looked astonished. "What makes you think that?"

"He threatened me on the mainland because he thought I saw him in the marsh near Michael's body. He drove up to the gate only minutes after I discovered the body. He works for you, Tom Murphy, Larry's Garage, Robert Davis, and I don't know who else. Joe, the security guard, I suppose. He knows everybody and every inch of this island. But why would he do it unless one of the people he works for paid him? I need to think about this."

Dickie shook his head. "Trust me. Toot ain't involved in this. He don't run around killing people. Neither does anybody else I know."

"Motive, Dickie," Maggie said. "Let's approach this from a logical standpoint, not an emotional one. Who knew Michael?"

"How should I know? I think we'd better stay out of it. I got the locks in my truck. We'll get this place secure, and you enjoy the rest of your vacation."

"We'll use the process of elimination. The killer is trying to scare me because he thinks I know more than I do. I've been over that murder scene a hundred times in my mind. I must have missed an important clue. Let's list suspects and put a motive with each one. We'll get to the bottom of this. I'll be able to hand this one to Hammond on a silver platter."

"Is this gonna be like Perry Mason?" Dickie asked with a grin.

"This is serious," Maggie said sternly, "real life. I'm approaching the murder from a practical, yet intellectual, aspect. Hammond doesn't understand this reasoning process."

"Well, neither do I," Dickie said. "But I like you, and you're sure easy on the eyes, and you've got this stubborn look on your face, so I guess I'll stick around and see what happens—as long as Sally Jo don't find out."

"We'll make a list," Maggie said. "I'll get a yellow pad and pen from the kitchen. Want a beer?"

"Sure thing," Dickie answered. "A bartender don't never turn down a free drink."

Maggie slammed the screen door and padded down the hallway to the kitchen. Sunlight scattered shadows from the open front door.

"Hey, Dickie, was the front door open when you drove up?" Maggie called.

No answer. The house was quiet. Maggie heard the condenser from the air conditioning unit pumping cold air from the house out the front door. "I'm cooling the entire island," she grumped out loud. She walked to the door and reached out to swing it closed. A dark shadow fell across her path.

"Dickie?" she said.

The black shadow jumped from behind the door. It jabbed her in the stomach, a hard, sharp chop. Maggie doubled over and fell on the floor. The shadow flew through the open doorway.

"Dickie," Maggie screamed, "help me!"

Dickie ran down the hall to Maggie. The portable phone was next to his ear.

"What happened?" he yelled. "No, Mister Heyward, not you. It's Maggie. She's on the floor holding her stomach. Okay, hang on." Dickie placed the phone on the floor and crouched by Maggie.

"He ran out the door. Go after him. I'm okay."

Dickie grabbed the phone and charged down the front steps. Maggie reached for the table to gain support and pulled herself up. She heard Dickie babbling into the phone as he cased the yard. Her stomach hurt. A wave of nausea swept over her. Another attack, but not serious. The attacker must have heard her conversation with Dickie. He was trying to find out how much she knew. He thought she was a threat.

Maggie examined her stomach. A bright blue bruise was taking shape just above her navel, a pretty match for the fading bruises on her legs. This confirmed that the attacker had a key. He must have made a copy, then replaced the original, leaving it on the kitchen counter. Was it Robert Davis or did she need a guest list from S.J.'s party? At least that would give her a start on suspects. This also proved that the killer and the attacker were the same person, she thought.

"Vanished," Dickie announced. "He musta been moving fast."

"He almost knocked the breath out of me. Same character that attacked before. You've been with me both times, but haven't seen him. You aren't leaving until you get these locks changed. Now!"

"Mister Heyward was on the phone when it happened. I guess you didn't hear the phone ring. He thinks you'd better spend the night at Seaward Inn. Give Hammond time to investigate. You just relax. I'll get us a beer and see if Billy has a room at the inn for to-night."

"Don't call Hammond yet. He'll just say the Black Plague is fol-lowing me. You change the locks and I'll stay at the inn tonight. What else did John say?"

Maggie gingerly stretched her body on the lounge chair. A night away from this house would give her a new perspective. Fresh sheets and room service, and she'd be able to put her suspects on paper. The pattern would emerge. This attacker wasn't trying to kill her. He only meant to frighten her, and he'd certainly done that, but she would not give up.

Maggie watched with relief as John bounded up the stairs.

"I was on the car phone with Dickie. You okay? Need a doctor? He answered when I called to discuss a time for dinner."

"Thank God you're here. I'm fine. I think I'll stay over at the inn tonight. Dickie's changing the locks before he leaves."

"Great. We'll do dinner there. Bring a dress. I'll meet you in the lobby at six-thirty." John reached out and put his hand on her arm. "Are you sure you're okay?" He leaned over. His clear blue eyes spar-kled. He moved his face closer, and then Dickie came bounding into the room, causing John to move a step back. She couldn't help but be disappointed. She had needed that kiss.

"Beer for everybody," Dickie said. "I got ya the honeymoon suite, top floor," he told Maggie. "You get a killer view of the Atlan-tic Ocean. Thanks for coming, Mister Heyward. I panicked when I saw her sprawled on the floor."

"See you in the lobby," John said. "Six-thirty. Stay here until she leaves, Dickie. Don't let her out of your sight." Maggie watched John until she couldn't see his car anymore.

Dickie flopped on the other lounge chair and took a hard pull on his Coors Light. "Cold beer, hot afternoon. Perfect," he said.

"I truly trust John," Maggie told Dickie. "His major transgression is knowing Alice. I guess he can't help that. Their families have always been close. What's the real story on Alice and Ralph?"

"You know how gossip runs at the Red-Eye. Mona, whose mama has always worked for them, says Ralph has a woman in New York. Alice found out. The other version is Alice is in love with a younger man on Seaward. Holy shit! Maggie, it just occurred to me. Was Alice having an affair with Michael? And she killed him because he was going to tell Ralph?"

"Dickie, please, you're sounding like an afternoon soap opera. Anyway, Alice was at the tennis court all afternoon. People saw her. She was waiting for John. I wish I could remember what the coroner said about time of death. I don't think he'd been dead very long when I found the body. That gives Alice her alibi, or does it? Maybe she told people that she was waiting on the court, but left, killed Michael, got back without being missed. But she's too tall to be my attacker unless... I do have another job for you after you change these locks this afternoon."

"What's that?"

"I want you to have a serious talk with Toot Sweet. Find out why he was at the gate right after the murder. Ask him about the security guard. The deliveries he makes, what are they? Hasn't he ever mentioned them to you?"

"Naw. Toot works for just about everybody. Says he's saving money to leave the island and move far away. Talks like that all the time. He's just running his mouth, but I'll see what I can find out." Dickie gave her a big grin. "Does this mean we're partners, you know, like Mason and Street? I can kinda tell Sally Jo we're just working on this. All right?"

Maggie couldn't help but smile at Dickie's enthusiasm. "Tell Sally Jo that you're an investigator. She'll like that."

107

"Yeah, good thinking. She's trying to get the fundraiser going for Saturday night. If we could get a bunch of tourists from the mainland over here, say five dollars a head, the Red-Eye'd make some money. Will ya talk to her 'bout it? She sure could use your ideas."

"She just needs to get the word out. I'll think of a way we can advertise. What if we got a local radio station to promote a Beach Float at Liberty Oak, The First Annual Spring Tide Celebration?"

"Wow, Maggie. Killer! I'll check with Billy at the inn. I think he knows a D.J. at ZQ-106. They could broadcast a remote. You a flat-out genius, Maggie. Gotta run. Get this shaking."

Maggie grabbed his arm. "Stop, Dickie. Priorities. Number one, change the locks. Number two, talk to Toot. But first drive me to the inn after I pack. I'm taking Possum with me. I'll sneak her in if I have to. If the Volvo is in the driveway and he comes back…"

"I gotcha. Well, get moving toward your luggage. I'm a man with a mission."

Maggie felt better already. Dinner with John. The honeymoon suite. Maybe she'd invite him up for a drink after dinner. Humming her mom's favorite song, "Some Enchanted Evening", she raced down the hall to pack her suitcase.

Fourteen

Click. Click. Polished marble tile echoed with the touch of Maggie's heels. The primary developers of Seaward Inn had indulged in opulence.

At two hundred twenty-five dollars a night, and extra for Possum's kennel in her room, Maggie hoped her attacker would be caught soon. At least she was protected for now. She ought to be at that outrageous rate.

The lobby imitated the style of a grand hotel of the 1930s. Perfect for an "escape from stress" weekend. Potted palms swayed in the cool of an air-conditioned breeze. Off the left of the lobby, a wide veranda beckoned toward the ocean. Windows across the back of the inn reflected a calmer spring tide. Silvery white waves splashed a gentle skirt around the outer edges of beach sand.

Maggie felt calmer, too. A long, gardenia-scented bubble bath restored her and helped to put thoughts into a more realistic perspective. Too damn many major variables in the death of a talented art student. Her list of suspects widened with each new thought. Dickie's job, after the change of door locks if he could follow through on that, would be implemented tomorrow. The suspect list and candidates for her attacker were the same. Tomorrow, she would take the time to examine closely the murder scene and the lagoon, relive the experience.

Six forty-five. Maggie looked around the lobby again. Two older ladies of the blue-hair brigade were perched on a lush velvet, hunter green sofa. Their backs straight, heads high, the pair chatted in hushed tones. Music from the big band era floated from the dining room into the lobby.

Maggie chose a green and burgundy plaid upholstered Queen Anne chair facing the ocean. She reached for the *Seaward Times,* a weekly tribute to the style of the island, but then she hesitated and didn't pick it up. She didn't want printer's ink all over her hands. John had called and said he'd meet her in the lobby at seven. Her mind began to drift again. Two years. Two years since her engagement to Bob Markham. After college, Bob's career had taken off immediately. Hers had not. Their relationship struggled through that last summer and died with the falling leaves. Bob had called a month ago to tell her that he was marrying the woman he'd been sleeping with while they were engaged. Her heart had not flip-flopped when she heard his voice. She had wished him well. A huge sigh filled her body and she released it into the cool lobby air.

"Thoughts that heavy?" John asked. He approached Maggie with a crystal blue sparkle in his eyes.

Maggie responded with her genuine smile. "Are we on for dinner in the dining room?" she asked.

"Seafood buffet and dancing until dawn." John grabbed Maggie's hand. Maggie clasped his fingers and took another deep breath. Falling in step beside him, she wanted to hum "Some Enchanted Evening".

And then Alice appeared. "John, darling, how clever of you to be on time. You said that you and Maggie would be here. I knew you'd want me to join you. Since Ralph left, I seem to have more free time," Alice said. She was leaning on the door frame to the dining room, waiting like a shark to advance upon its prey in the briny stench of a polluted sea.

Maggie continued to hold John's hand. Alice clutched his other arm and pulled them into the dining room. The two ladies from the lobby tottered behind them into the dining room, giggling to each other. Maggie stared at John. Why had he told Alice where they'd be?

John averted his eyes from Maggie's glare and turned toward the waiter at the door. "Mister Heyward, your table is right this way. Follow me."

Alice managed to squeeze herself into the seat between Maggie and John. The view of the ocean from their table was extraordinary. Maggie ignored Alice and concentrated on her surroundings. This overdone, but half-baked brassy bitch continued to dominate the conversation.

"I had a most interesting talk with S.J. after the memorial service," Alice told John. "She called. Wanted my opinion of the service, I'm sure. She was carrying on about how much we'd miss Michael, not that any of us even knew him, what a great student he was. I told her you thought Robert Davis was the killer. She was appalled."

"I never said that," Maggie said.

"You certainly implied that, my dear. Running after him down the beach. I'm glad we didn't catch him. He would have thought you'd lost it, Maggie."

"And I suppose you had an explanation for running down the beach with me."

"I write 'Island Talk' for the *Seaward T1mes*. I always have a reason for being where I am, darling. John, dear me, you're just too quiet tonight."

"The waiter wants your drink orders. Maggie, what'll it be?" John asked.

"Gin and tonic."

"I'll have the same," Alice added. "I'm still trying to assimilate S.J.'s ramblings from our phone conversation. The shock of Michael's death hasn't worn off. She literally sounded like a basket case. Perhaps you'd better check on her tomorrow, Maggie. She is your neighbor, after all."

Only for this vacation, Maggie thought.

The waiter approached with their drinks, thankfully eliminating a response from Maggie. He placed the drinks on the table and leaned over to Alice. "Telephone at the front desk," he said.

Alice stopped her dissertation in mid-sentence. "Must be Ralph. He's been calling constantly since last night, you know. Now don't go away, dears, I'll be right back." Alice grabbed her purse and drink and flounced across the dining room. Everyone's eyes followed her out the door. A chilly fog lifted from the atmosphere. To Maggie, the room turned warm and cozy.

"Maggie," John said in a very quiet voice, "thank you. She's having a hard time now and needs support. I think she wants to get back with Ralph. She's a real insecure person. I've told you before she and I have been friends for a long, long time. Have patience for a little longer. Maybe she and Ralph will move back to Connecticut. It would be good for their marriage to be away from here."

John shifted his position and looked directly into Maggie's eyes. "Are you settled in here? I've heard the top suite has a sweeping view of Seaward and the Atlantic Ocean."

"You'll have to judge for yourself. Maybe we'll have a nightcap at the end of this evening, that is if Possum hasn't torn the place apart. She's kenneled, but I can't remember if I fastened the latch."

"Whoa. The inn let you bring a dog in here? Or did you and Dickie sneak her in?"

"Almost. Dickie wanted me to distract the desk clerk while he shoved Possum's cage into the elevator. I refused. I've never been able to get away with murder. Oops. Poor choice of words. That's the last subject I want to discuss. I worked out a deal with the manager. I told him I would not only pay for damages, if there are any, but also use my designing expertise. I almost hope we have some damage. It would be more challenging than the Rosemont clients."

"You need a change, Maggie. I'm not trying to tell you what to do, but it does sound like, from what you've told me, you don't need to spend the rest of your life there. But a bigger city may not be the answer. How about a small shop over on the mainland? You could do houses and condos all over the coastal Carolina area."

"My degree was in classical design, and I've always worked with traditional, but I've never had the opportunity, except the Meyers' house, to implement ideas and designs. Interesting. I'll at least add that to my 'what am I gonna be when I grow up' list." Before John could respond, the waiter approached the table.

"Mister Heyward, the lady who went out for her phone call asked me to bring this note to you."

John unfolded the inn stationery and read the note, folded it, and put it in his jacket pocket.

"It's a note from Alice. She's gone on a mission of mercy. Doesn't really explain."

"Mission of mercy?" Maggie asked.

"Alice is rather dramatic. She'll have a clever story when she returns," John answered.

"Maybe she won't come back," Maggie said.

"Don't count on it. She'll come sailing in, breathless, with the dessert. All sweets and apologies for leaving us."

Twilight crept into the dining room. Alice had been gone for over an hour. Gray mist rolled onto the island. There were at least two or three people on the beach, but they were too far away to be recognized in the haze. The band began a lively rendition of Cole Porter classics.

"Come on, let's dance," John said. "We can boogie with the best of these old folks. After all, we're at least half their age."

Maggie laughed and swung into his arms as they glided across the floor.

"Finally, my vacation dream is coming true. Until now it's been a nightmare," she said. John squeezed her as he brought her to him after a quick twirl.

113

"I'm sorry you've gotten the wrong impression of our quiet island. Did you see the headlines in the afternoon *Seaward Times* edition? Hammond arrested Toot Sweet. I still can't believe Toot did it. He swears he didn't. What I can't figure out is, if he was in jail, who broke into your house this afternoon and why?"

"Toot arrested?" Maggie stopped in the middle of the dance floor. "You're positive? Dickie didn't even know that this afternoon. He would have told me. I thought the sheriff had checked him out a few days ago."

"I've tried to reach Hammond. Hope he'll call back soon. Let's eat. It looks like Alice isn't going to be back for dinner after all. After we eat, we'll dance some more."

The buffet was laden with oysters, scallops, crab cakes, and shrimp. Maggie piled her plate with a little bit of it all.

"It'll be dark after dinner. Let's take a moonlight walk down the beach and look for the turtles. It may be a week or two early, but we can try," John said.

"Turtles?" Maggie said, as she plunked a succulent shrimp into her mouth.

"They come every year around spring tide to lay their eggs. Those turtles are so big, you could ride on their backs. A beautiful sight."

"Will they continue to come if the island is over-developed?"

"Hopefully the development will continue to be controlled. Remember, most of my family's holdings on the island are going to be maintained as a wildlife preserve. I'm trying to talk Alice into doing the same. If Ralph ever gets half of it, he'll put pressure on the state legislature to build a bridge from the mainland and put up houses and condos faster than you can pass go. Alice only says that's what she wants to please Ralph."

The waiter interrupted their conversation. "Mister Heyward, the sheriff's in the lobby. He asked me to come get you."

"At last! We'll find out about Toot. Be right back." John excused himself and walked out to the lobby.

Maggie took the final bite of her Shrimp Allston. Delicious. The chef had probably used white wine instead of sherry. Granny Jenkins, her mother's cook, had always used sherry and measured with a wine glass. She'd sip and pour. That shrimp recipe was almost as good as her tipsy pudding.

John came running back to the table.

"Stay in the hotel. Go up to your room and lock the door. Don't let anyone in. Get the waiter to take you up. Have him check the room before you go in." John was out of breath and clearly agitated.

Maggie stared at him. "Do what?"

"A tourist found Alice's body floating in the shallows of the outgoing tide in front of this hotel. Just a while ago. Hammond came immediately. She's wearing a damn red ribbon around her neck."

And then John was gone.

Maggie fixed her eyes on her empty plate as if she'd never seen it. Alice dead. She had wished Alice would go away, but she certainly hadn't wanted that. Tears sprang to her eyes. "Dead," Maggie mumbled. "But why her and not me? Or am I next?"

The waiter began to clear the table. The band packed its instruments, while the dining room emptied. Guests left the lobby and headed toward the beach in groups to gape at the ugly spectacle. Maggie headed toward the elevator. The thought of Alice lying dead on that hard, sandy beach made Maggie gag.

She turned and pressed the arrow button for UP on the elevator. The door swished open. Maggie walked into the car, her head down, her thoughts on Alice, and pressed the button for her floor. The door slid closed.

Maggie turned and stood face-to-face with Toot Sweet.

Fifteen

Floor-to-ceiling mirrors reflected the wild look in Toot's eyes. Maggie grabbed the elevator handrail. Her mouth opened and closed, but the scream stuck in her throat. Toot leaned over and pushed the STOP button. A whiff of alcohol and dead shrimp assaulted Maggie's nostrils. She gagged. The elevator screeched and jolted to a stop between floors. Toot kept his greasy finger on the button.

"What did you tell the po-lice about me? I warned you before not to get me in trouble," he said.

Maggie gasped and tried to make her mouth work. "How did you get out of jail?" she sputtered.

"The sheriff let me go. You lying bitch. I didn't attack you. I ain't hurt nobody." Toot leaned over toward Maggie. She cringed. "Why does Hammond keep asking me about that artsy-fartsy art student?"

"You were there, near the scene, remember? You drove up to the gate right after I discovered the body. Bad move, Toot. You left a cryptic message for the security guard. Are you two partners? Which one of you killed Alice? She died just a few yards from here, and now you turn up. That's quite a coincidence."

Toot jerked his finger away from the button. The elevator jerked again and glided toward Maggie's floor. Toot covered his face with his hands and moaned. "Oh, my God! I ain't kilt nobody!"

The elevator door opened. Both passengers barged out at the same time. The force of their bodies knocked over a woman waiting to go down. Toot stepped on the hem of her dress as he jumped over her. His other foot crushed the evening bag next to her right arm. Maggie bolted down the corridor toward her room. The

woman was gathering the contents of her purse and mumbling obscenities about today's youth.

Maggie stopped in mid-stride. Toot wasn't chasing her. He had
fled the other way, down the emergency stairs. She rushed to her
room door. Hammond could catch him if he was still on the beach.
Toot had given her another warning, tried to intimidate her, but he
didn't try to kill her. His reaction was strange when she mentioned
Alice. Her hand shook as she inserted the key card. Jerking the
phone off the hook, Maggie punched the front desk.

"This is Ms. Stewart in the honeymoon suite. Please get a message to Sheriff Hammond quickly. I need to talk to him immediately. My life's in danger." After gently replacing the phone, she ran
across the plush Oriental rug and willed herself to breathe slowly.
Inching the door to her bedroom open, she peeked in. No one was
there but Possum, curled into a fluffy yellow ball in the middle of
her kennel cage. Her toys were scattered around the cage. She slept
as peacefully as a full puppy next to a mother's tit.

The view from the glass window, touted as the most beautiful on
the eastern seaboard, showed spotlights and blue police car lights cir-
cling the beach. If Toot was innocent, she thought...and he could
be. Otherwise, she'd be dead or his hostage instead of viewing this
gory scene spread in front of her. From this height and angle, the ee-
rie lights and people on the beach looked like giant crabs dancing
themselves into a frenzy. She turned away from the window, sank
onto the sofa and willed her heart to stop beating rapidly. Why did-
n't Toot at least explain why he'd been looking for Joe? Was Joe a
major suspect? He had been near the scene, and he had ample opportunity to kill and return to his post at the gate. Means, opportunity,
but no motive. He'd warned Maggie to stay away from the lagoon;
she'd thought he was being a smart-ass. Maybe he didn't want her
to find Michael's body. If he were guilty, did Robert Davis fit into it

at all? He was smaller than Joe and fit the frame of her attacker. Joe was too tall and thin.

A loud knock caused Maggie's heart to beat rapidly again. "Who's there?" she stammered.

"Ken Hammond." "John." The men spoke simultaneously.

Maggie unbolted the lock and eased the chain off. John burst in, grabbed her and hugged her fiercely.

"Toot Sweet trapped me in the elevator. It was so scary. But he didn't try to touch me. When the elevator stopped, he ran the other way. How'd he know I was at the inn? Why didn't he try to kill me?" Maggie sobbed and held tightly to John. She felt a strong reassurance from his hug.

"We know. Sit down," the sheriff said. "We caught Toot running out the side door. First thing he said was, 'I didn't touch Miss Stewart.' Anyway, he was free because we didn't have enough evidence to hold him. And I know he wasn't involved in Alice's murder because he was with me until just before I got the call that she had been found on the beach. Damn fool Sherman Prichard at the *Seaward Times* had his hearing aid off and screwed up another story. He sent his scoop to press with Toot as the killer. Maybe he'll retire after this fiasco.

"It does buy me some time, though, if the killer thinks he's got away with it. Sure can't figure how Alice fits into all this."

He glanced at Maggie and saw she was still trembling. "Sorry, I'm thinking out loud. Toot's granny wants you to drop by and see her. I told her that I'd give Miss Maggie the message."

The sheriff looked at John, then Maggie, and leered.

Maggie stepped away from John. The heat from her flushed face felt like a sunburn. "See ya'll later." Hammond closed the door. Maggie heard his heavy footsteps plodding toward the elevator. She turned around and hugged John again.

"I'm sorry about Alice," she said.

"Let's order from room service. I never finished dinner." John picked up the phone and ordered food and drinks. "Time to talk. I'm truly upset about Alice, but I want you to understand about her. You're going to hear a lot of wild stories in the next few days. I want you to hear the truth from me."

"Understand what?"

"My relationship with Alice. It goes back a long way. I may have told you that she and my sister were roommates at Hollins. When Catherine died, I wanted Alice to take my sister's place. She always wanted more than that. Her marriage to Ralph was done in haste and probably spite. It was a disaster. Ralph is in New York talking to his attorney about a legal separation. Alice and I were discussing that while you were lurking in the bushes at S.J.'s party."

"You saw me?"

"Yes, but Alice didn't. She was afraid that her daughter, Jane, from a previous marriage would find out from Ralph about the separation. She wanted me to talk to Jane, go to her boarding school in Connecticut. Jane always hated Ralph, but Alice thought that Jane would feel she was a failure to have had three husbands already."

"What about you and Alice? Did she plan for you to be number four?"

A knock at the door made Maggie jump. A voice from the other side of the door called, "Room service." The conversation had become so intense, she'd forgotten where she was.

John helped the waiter set up the table and pour wine. He tipped him and closed the door. Maggie accepted her glass. She felt his fingers touch hers in a smooth caress.

"Four's not a good number for me. Let's sit on the balcony and relax with our wine," he said.

"This afternoon, when Dickie told me he had reservations, he said I'd have a killer view," Maggie said. "That's been haunting me."

"It is beautiful out there now. Quiet, too. See the light at the edge of the island? That's the twelve-mile light, a warning for ships. I wonder if Alice had a warning. I'm positive she knew her killer. She wouldn't have sent me that note if she'd been frightened."

A cool, slow, spring breeze blew fitfully off the ocean. Maggie looked up at the stars and back into John's clear blue eyes. "The truth," Maggie said.

"The shock is wearing off." John took a large sip of wine. "For the last time, we were friends. Nothing more, at least on my part. It's been a long time since I've really thought about a serious relationship."

"Me, too," Maggie said.

"Alice wanted people to think we were having an affair. She was so insecure. She knew no one on the island would tell Ralph. He spent a lot of her money on other women. She had faults, too, but I'll always remember the fun times we... I hope they catch the bastard that killed her, soon."

"Maybe Toot Sweet isn't guilty, at least not of murder. He's got the best alibi of all. He was with Hammond. And if he'd killed Michael, he'd have strangled me in that elevator. Did Alice ever discuss Michael's death with you?"

"Not really. She didn't know him."

"But she knew something. The murderer knew she knew enough to incriminate him. The phone call, was it a man or a woman? It had to have been the murderer luring her to the beach."

"The front desk couldn't say."

"I'm trying not to feel guilty," Maggie said. "I was elated when Alice left, and I didn't want her to come back. Okay, I confess. I wanted to spend time with you, just the two of us."

John smiled. "More wine?"

"Let's finish the bottle while we eat. It's after midnight. Your supper is probably cold."

"I ordered cold," John said. "Hope you like it. Snow peas stuffed with herb cheese, hickory smoked trout, shrimp piquant, and small, soft rolls at room temperature for the tenderloin with horseradish sauce."

"Gorgeous. Looks like a cocktail party."

"It was. The Gilberts' party. Sorry we weren't invited. I told the kitchen to send up leftovers from their major evening event. I've always wanted to pull up a chair, get a dinner plate, and eat everything in sight at one of those stuffy affairs. You stand around the table, never get enough to eat. About the time you manage to get crab-dip crackers in your mouth, the bank president walks up and asks, 'How's business?' "

"After spitting crab dip all over his silk tie, you know you'd never have a snowball's chance of the loan you want," Maggie said. "Let's have music with dinner."

Maggie set the dial of the room's stereo system to public radio. "Tales of the Vienna Woods" floated across the table. Silently, they munched their food and drank the wine. John broke the spell with a quiet thought.

"Yes, I'll miss Alice, but she was just a friend. A more profound relationship wouldn't have worked for us. Understand?"

"Yes, I do."

"I'm glad you're here," John said, reaching across the table to take her hand. "Ralph's plane lands at nine this morning. I told him I'd meet him at the airport. It was hard as hell to talk to him over Hammond's car phone."

Maggie squeezed his hand. "So much has happened since I arrived," she said. "I came to house-sit and have a vacation. Instead, I've become involved in murder, acquired a dog, and made no decisions about staying in Rosemont or going to a bigger city or just throwing it all away and becoming a Seaward beach bum. Bet Dickie would give me a job waiting tables at the Red-Eye, but I'd probably have to buy the tables and decorate the place. No income future there. And I'd be the first Red-Eye waitress not to have blood-shot eyes, just chicken pox."

John laughed. "Thanks for helping me calm down and put some perspective on tonight's horror. I want you to spend all long week-ends on Seaward this summer. I hope you'll want to."

He pushed his chair back and walked around the table to Mag-gie. He pulled her gently to her feet. The sound of Strauss waltzes filled the silence. He drew her close and smiled into her questioning eyes.

Sixteen

Gray, gritty, salty water. Torrential force of never-ending waves splashing over and over her head. The sea was pulling her to the bottom. Red ribbons slapped through the surf, hitting her face and neck. Struggling, gasping for air, Maggie managed to shake herself awake. She was safe and free from the gripping nightmare.

The place next to her in bed was empty. John had slept on the sofa. The clock blinked seven-thirty a.m. Untangling herself from the sweaty sheets, Maggie reached for her robe and headed for the shower. John had managed to sneak out early to catch the first run of the *Mary Grace*. The phone rang. She snatched the receiver on the second ring.

"Hammond here. Dickie changed the locks on your doors. I'm leaving the new keys at the front desk. Pick 'em up when you check out."

The sheriff paused, and then said in a somber tone, "You need to continue to be careful. Are you sure you can't remember anything else?"

Maggie sighed. "No. I wish I could forget it. I've been having nightmares since it happened."

"I'm sorry," Hammond replied. "By the way, call your neighbor, S.J. She's been looking for you. Says you can stay with her. She sounded worried about you. I told her you're okay. You are, aren't you?"

"Yes. Why?"

"Well, John's Mercedes was still there after I left the inn about three-thirty this morning, but I noticed it wasn't in the parking lot just now."

"He's meeting Ralph's plane on the mainland this morning. Thanks, I'll remember the new keys."

Maggie cradled the receiver with a strong thud. The absolute nerve of that man! He implied that he knew John had spent the night. The entire island was probably standing in the inn's parking lot, ready to pounce for the gossip when she emerged. Small island with jungle drums. S.J. probably knew it all by now, but she'd stop by on her way back to the beach house. Once more she headed toward the shower. She'd have to remember to call Marilyn and Greg about the locks. She didn't want them to have to break into their own home when they returned. A loud knock interrupted her thoughts.

"What now?" she said to herself, and then called, "Who's there?"

"Maggie, it's me, Dickie. I come to take you home. Mister Heyward asked me to."

"I'm not ready," she answered. "Take Possum and her kennel for me. Meet me in the dining room. We'll have breakfast. Twenty minutes."

Twenty-five minutes later, Maggie placed her travel bag by the table. New keys jangled in the pocket of her white duck pants.

"That's your breakfast, Dickie? Three sweet rolls, apple pastry, a Danish, and what's that dark glob on the other side of your plate?"

"Sorry. I ain't never eat in a place like this. I'm trying one of everything. Sally Jo would love it. 'Course, she'd have to take off her pink rollers. None of them blue-haired old ladies are wearing them. Their hair is already curly enough, I guess."

Maggie hid her smile and ordered her usual breakfast, toasted wheat bread and coffee. "We've got work to do, Dickie."

Dickie looked up at her through perpetually smudged glasses, chewing a mouthful of sweet roll. "We do?"

"We're going to gather evidence, tie it all up." Maggie stopped, deep in thought. "The red ribbon. It's a major clue."

Dickie grinned. "It is?"

"Bring your Danish with you. We're visiting the murder scene, now." Maggie dropped money on the table, picked up her bag, and headed for the front door. Dickie scrambled to grab as much food as he could and followed.

"Possum's waiting for us in the truck," he said.

Maggie wasn't listening. She kept talking as she walked through the dining room. "It's the same killer. Got to be. And that killer thinks I know enough to keep warning me away. Are you coming?" Maggie glanced over her shoulder as she walked down the front steps of the inn. Then she burst into laughter.

Dickie seemed to be caught in the revolving door. The Danish pastry was smashed between his nose and the glass. The harder he pushed, the faster the door spun. Maggie ran back and extracted him from his rotating prison before he was ejected into orbit.

"That's a tricky damn contraption," he said, looking dizzy. "I always go through the back door of the inn. People I know here work in the back."

Dickie wiped his face with a soiled, white handkerchief.

"We're wasting time," Maggie said impatiently. "We'll stop off at the security gate on the way to the lagoon. I want to talk to Joe. I hope he's working this morning. Is Possum okay in her cage back there? I'd rather she'd be up here with us."

"Ain't enough room."

Dickie put his Chevy pickup in reverse and moved slowly away from the inn. Maggie saw only two other cars on the road. That was part of the beauty of Seaward. It was almost impossible to get a car over here on the ferry. It cost big bucks.

"Do you think Seaward will ever have a bridge?" she asked.

"Naw. Mainland taxpayers would have to help foot the bill. They're more interested in education right now. We're safe for a few more years, unless some big developer built it hisself. I bet Mister Heyward would try to stop that. Of course, Alice's husband, Ralph, may have the money now. We'll see. But a bridge would shore help my business at the Red-Eye."

"A coat of paint would help business at the Red-Eye," Maggie said with a laugh.

"Yeah. I plum forgot to tell you: Sally Jo's really excited 'bout the fundraiser Saturday night. She liked the Beach Float theme. Hope you don't mind, but I kinda told her it was my idea. We need to make some more plans 'bout that. Will ya help us?"

"You help me gather evidence, and I'll help you with Saturday. Maybe I'll even donate money, to compensate for the time you're spending helping me. Deal?"

"You betcha."

The pickup stopped at the security gate. An unfamiliar guard stepped up.

"Morning. Hey, hey, Dickie. Where ya been? Little Lavender was a-giving away freebies at the bar last night. Said ya told him to lock up and tend bar. So he locked everybody in, and we had ourselves a blast. Ya shoulda been there."

"Oh, hell. Excuse me, Maggie, but that idiot would starch a laundry list. I gotta get me some better help." Dickie continued to mumble profanities.

"Where's Joe?" Maggie asked.

"Don't know," the guard replied. "I heard he was taking a few days off 'til it gets a little cooler. It don't seem no hotter now than it was this time last year, you think?"

"Does Joe live on the island, Dickie?" Maggie asked. "We need to find him right now."

"What's the rush?" the guard asked.

Maggie and Dickie ignored him. Dickie backed the truck and made a wide U-turn in the road.

"Later, man," the guard called after them.

"Joe's been staying in that old building that used to be called Shipyard Marina. 'Bout twenty years ago, it was the only place on Seaward where you could get boat gas. Then the ferry changed its route and started going to Markley's Landing. Shipyard went out of business. Joe said that the rent was so cheap, he couldn't afford to move. If this is gonna help our investigation, then I'm a-gonna take you there right now," Dickie said.

"He may be up to his eyeballs in murder. Do you know who Robert Davis is?"

"He's that new man on the island that was at the memorial service? Some friend of Miss Styles?"

"I think so."

"Sally Jo said she heard he might buy the Shipyard Marina and fix it up. Could just be talk."

"Wait a minute, Dickie. That would link Davis with the security guard. Hurry! We need to get there fast."

"But I thought you wanted to look for clues at the lagoon."

"If we find Joe, maybe we won't need any clues. Can't you make this jalopy go faster?"

Dickie slapped his foot to the floor and uttered a string of obscenities. The truck seemed to jump forward.

"I apologize. I don't mean to cuss in front of you, but it shore makes this truck go faster. Sally Jo says I'm to always behave proper-like with a lady. You won't tell her, will ya? You don't think I'm awful, do you?"

Maggie laughed. "You would be appalled at some of the language I've listened to while decorating ladies' estates. I've heard it all. But thanks for calling me a lady. I haven't heard that in a long time. This island seems to have a code of its own. I bet a lot of oral history has been passed through generations."

"You need to hear some of the stories Granny Jones tells about long time ago on these islands. She's Toot's granny, by the way.

She's real good buddies with Mister Heyward. He likes to go over to her trailer and visit with her. He even paid for that doublewide to be brought over here. He said if that's what she wanted, then she ought to have it.

"He's good to everybody, even an aggravatin' woman like Alice. Guess I shouldn't speak ill of the dead. That's another rule Sally Jo learned me."

"Will you take me over to meet Granny Jones before I leave? I'd really like to learn more about this part of our state from people who've lived here."

"Be glad to. Wanna go now?"

"Don't try to sidetrack me, Dickie. We're not in any danger. We're just going to find out what happened to Joe. You're not afraid, are you?"

"Me? No way. I'm more scared of Sally Jo's mama. She says she gonna shoot me if I don't marry her daughter soon. Wants us to move to the mainland, get better jobs. Wants me to make something of myself. I just want to be proprietor of the Red-Eye."

"Dickie, I've always thought that a person should be true to themselves first. Hold out for the Red-Eye if that's what you want. You've mentioned that Sally Jo is jealous. Does she know you're running around the island with me?"

"Not exactly. I told her that I'm doing some work for Mister Heyward. He did ask me to keep an eye on you when I saw him this morning—er—in the parking lot."

"You and everybody else on the island saw him leave my room this morning."

Dickie flushed a bright red and turned the truck into a deserted, muddy parking lot paved with oyster shells instead of asphalt. "Looks like ain't nobody here," he said, sounding relieved.

"I guess we're too late. Joe's long gone. Let's get out and look around anyway."

130

The cinder block building stood alone at the front of the lot. Trash and beer bottles were piled near the front door. The entire area was treeless and desolate. A wooden dock with boards missing jutted out from the marina.

The paint on a metal sign lying on the ground next to the dock had eroded away. It might have said "Shipyard Marina" years ago. Pilings under the dock creaked as the tide ebbed from the shore. Maggie was the first to spot the boat.

"Dickie, that's the same boat, the *Boston Whaler,* the one I've seen before. Come on. We need to take a closer look."

"Look, there's a searchlight on the bow, the kind that alligator poachers use to hunt at night," Dickie said. "Hammond's been looking for alligator poachers for months. Before the murder, that's all he ever did."

Maggie grabbed Dickie's arm and headed down the muddy bank.

"Since no one's around, we can get proof for Hammond," Maggie said. "Maybe Michael found out about this and the poachers killed him to shut him up. If they're making a lot of money, then keeping Michael quiet would be a strong motive."

"Careful, Maggie. This oyster bed can cut you to ribbons."

"Ribbons!" Maggie said. "I've still got to figure out why they'd use red ribbon. And how Alice fits into all this."

Dickie tiptoed cautiously behind Maggie. A buzz zinged past his ear. He slapped at it.

"Damn mosquitoes. We're gonna get eaten alive. Let's go back and call Hammond. Let him do this. He ain't gonna like it when he finds out we investigated this boat."

"Quit complaining. They may come back and move the boat. He'd never find it again. He'll thank us for doing this."

The next zing hit the oyster shells between Maggie and Dickie. They realized that bullets were hitting on both sides of them.

"Somebody inside the building is shooting at us!" Dickie screamed. "Get down now!"

He and Maggie fell onto the ground.

"Crawl toward the boat and into the water," Maggie whispered in Dickie's ear. "We'll be safe there. Hold your breath and swim underwater to the other side of the boat. When I say three, let's go for it."

"I can't swim," Dickie wailed.

"You live on an island and you've never learned to swim?"

"Sally Jo and her mama are haunting me. That's what this is. Please God, get me outta this and I'll marry Sally Jo."

"Hush. Be still and let me think. I guess I'll have to pull you through the water to the other side of the boat. Wait, I hear a car motor."

Maggie raised her head from the ground and looked toward the parking lot. Toot Sweet's rusted green Cadillac spun out and headed down the road. The gunshots had stopped. It was quiet except for a sea gull's screech. Maggie jumped up. Dickie began to move on his hands and knees toward his pickup.

"Think we're safe now?" he asked after a moment. "I reckon I was just kiddin' about marrying Sally Jo."

"We'll discuss that later. Let's go get Hammond. Where do you think he'd be now?"

They stood up and looked at each other. Dickie's pants were ripped, and gray mud clung to his hair and body. Maggie's white pants had turned a brackish gray. A trickle of blood ran down her right arm. Cuts and scratches covered her arms.

"At least we weren't shot," she said.

Then they heard the sound of a vehicle approaching, and they stared at each other in horror.

"Oh, my God. The truck. He's coming back to finish us off!" Dickie screamed. They both fell face first back into the mud.

"Now, what can we do?" Maggie said. "We're halfway between the building and the boat."

It was quiet again. The engine stopped. Heavy footsteps began running toward them. Maggie lifted her face from the mud. The early morning dream of waves washing over her raced through her mind. She stared ahead. At least she would look the killer straight in the eyes.

"This time I mean it, Lord. Save me and I'll truly marry Sally Jo," Dickie shouted toward heaven.

Maggie looked up, straight into John's worried blue eyes. She jumped up, ran toward him, and fell into his arms. Mud and sand clung to his navy blue blazer as they hugged each other tightly.

"Every time I rescue you, you've just fallen into a pile of it. What this time?" he said.

Seventeen

" It's a damn good thing I missed my flight and can't leave 'til this afternoon. You're both crazy. Damn it, you could have been killed," John said. He turned to Dickie, glaring. "I told you to look after Maggie, not get in trouble with her. If I had decided to stay on the mainland instead of coming back, then you'd probably be dead. Thank God that new gate attendant remembered where you said you were going. Hell, I can't believe either of you!"

Maggie and Dickie sat on the deck glider at the beach house, their heads down. John fumed on a chair opposite the pair. Maggie had showered; Dickie had not. She tried, inconspicuously, to move away from him.

"How could we know what we were going to find?" she asked John. "Besides, if the shooter had wanted to kill us, he could have. The bullets were wide of their mark. It wasn't Michael's killer. He whacks his victims on the head and strangles with red ribbon. It was a warning to stay away from that boat. It would have happened to anyone going near it. Hammond even agreed with that."

At the mention of the sheriff's name, Dickie grimaced. "I'm damn glad he left. He shore asked enough questions. Maybe we really helped him. I bet by now he's got his alligator poachers."

"Hammond's looking for Joe, too. The Seaward Security Service said he was supposed to be at work this morning," John said.

"Joe is one of them poachers. I'd bet anything on that. I just don't know if Toot's involved. I hope not," Dickie said.

"He's got to be," Maggie said. "The first day I was here, Toot asked me to give Joe a message, something about deliveries. Alligator hides, I'll bet. And Joe didn't want me to go near the lagoon. He tried to scare me away. I'll just bet he was waiting for the boat to come trap the lagoon 'gator. And Michael saw them. They had to kill him."

"With red ribbon?" Dickie asked. "Never in my wildest dreams did I imagine poachers runnin' around with red satin ribbon."

John nodded. "Yeah, Dickie, 'gator poachers don't wear red ribbons," he said.

"Then who does?" Maggie demanded in exasperation. "And how does Alice's death fit into this?"

John shook his head and glanced at his Rolex.

"I've got a plane to catch," he said. "It took longer than I thought to get Hammond and answer his questions. I'm going to the mainland airport." He looked at both of them sternly. "May I trust you'll stay here? At least until you hear from Hammond. If he doesn't pick up the poachers, they may be after you. And call S.J. She phoned twice while you were in the shower. Wants to know details, I guess. Now listen up, Dickie." John gave Dickie a hard stare. "Stay with Maggie until I come back, you hear?"

"Yes, sir." Dickie hung his head again. Sand and mud fell onto his jeans and spattered on the deck.

John leaned over and kissed Maggie on the cheek.

"Thanks," Maggie said. "We'll be fine. If we hear from Hammond, we'll let you know."

Maggie heard John's Mercedes pull out of the driveway. She stood and stared at the ocean, her arms wrapped tightly around her upper body. Dickie stared at her. "Can we go over to my place? I mean, I need to clean up, change clothes and all. I'm beginning to smell myself."

"Go on. I'll make a few phone calls. Greg and Marilyn need to know I changed the locks on the door. I'll wait here until I hear from Hammond."

"Ain't no way I'm leaving you. Guess I'll stay this way forever."

136

"Okay. We'll go, but we need to be back in about twenty minutes. We don't want to upset John again."

"No problem. I'll drop you at the Red-Eye, then go to my place and change. Nobody can hurt you with all my friends around."

"It seems to me that Toot's a friend of yours. But I guess he could have hurt me in the elevator if he'd wanted to. Maybe he'll be there, and I'll have a chance to talk to him."

Maggie rolled the truck window down as they pulled out of the driveway.

"Toot said something about helping his granny this morning at the vegetable co-op," Dickie said. "He should be back at the Red-Eye by now. They sell crops at the ferry stand, had a good spring crop 'cause of our warm weather. If Joe's disappeared, he won't be helping Toot no more."

"Joe helped Toot at the vegetable co-op?"

"Yeah. Toot had to remind him all the time to pick up his share. Everybody in the program gets to take some home."

"Oh, Dickie, could that be what the message at the gate meant the first day I was here? Toot was reminding Joe to get his vegetables? Why didn't someone tell me that? That jerk Hammond. Maybe Joe isn't one of the poachers, or Toot. I'm so confused."

"You ain't the only one. All I know is someone's after you. We don't know why. You don't have proof of any of this. Let Hammond take care of it. I'll clean up and be back to get you right soon."

The Chevy truck pulled into the bar parking lot. A crowd of regulars had congregated in front of the Red-Eye. Maggie hopped out of the truck and began inching her way through. "What's going on?" she asked.

Country music from a radio floated out the bar door, and people around her were swaying to the music. In the center of the crowd, a torn mattress rested on the gravel lot. Buckets of sand had been scattered around the mattress and a middle-aged man in neon shorts sat cross-legged on the bedding. A cooler with cold beer was within reach of his right hand.

"Junior Tidwell's started his summer tan early this year," someone replied.

"But why doesn't he go over to the beach?" Maggie asked.

"No way, man. He's scairt of the ocean. Ain't been near it since he fell outta his pappy's fishing boat when he was twelve. But he likes to pretend he's at the beach."

"That man hasn't been off this island since he was twelve?"

Maggie shook her head in disbelief and walked inside the Red-Eye. Nothing had changed since her first visit, except a few more people were sitting at the bar, drinking in the middle of the day. She felt her eyes adjust to the darkness. The quartet from Michael's memorial service was practicing in the far corner of the room. Three men and a young woman with plastic pink rollers in her hair were sitting on bar stools.

"Dickie told me to wait here for him," Maggie told the woman, assuming she was Sally Jo. Dickie had said something about pink rollers, and how many women still wore them? "I'm Maggie Stewart. He's gone to shower."

The woman glared at Maggie. "Least you didn't shower with him. He's mine, you know. Mama and me are already planning the wedding. Think about that, Miss Smart-Ass Decorator."

Yep, Maggie thought, this is definitely Sally Jo.

A man Maggie didn't recognize came to her defense. "Little Lavender, give Maggie a beer. Sally Jo, Dickie's been working for her to make the money to pay for your wedding."

Little Lavender popped the top on a can of Coors Light. "This is the only brand we got," he said. "Ferry'll bring more today. Hope Toot remembers to pick it up."

"It's great. Thanks," Maggie said.

138

She slipped onto the stool next to Sally Jo and felt the ice cold beer hit her empty stomach. Little Lavender stood behind the bar. He had to be six-feet-four at least, and he was skinny as a rail. He wore a purple bandana on his head and a pale violet shirt unbuttoned at the neck. Gold chains flopped against his chest as he straightened the counter. Better not to ask about his name, Maggie thought.

The radio continued to play, and the band tried to follow the tune. Maggie thought this was a strange way to learn new songs. Occasionally, the musicians managed to hit a chord that matched one on the radio.

Sally Jo lit a cigarette and blew the smoke toward Maggie.

"Where's Toot Sweet? Isn't he supposed to be here?" Maggie asked her.

"Hell, Dickie leaves him in charge and the rascal ain't been here in two days. Heard he mighta been arrested. Why you asking?" Terrance, a Red-Eye regular, said.

"I wanted to ask him some questions. Sheriff Hammond's interrogated him, but there could be more."

"It's plum horrible," another customer spoke up. "Granny Jones says a serial killer could be loose on this island."

"What kinda cereal? Snap, crackle, pop, you're dead?" Little Lavender said.

Maggie groaned at his bad joke. Then she realized he was serious. No one else seemed to notice.

The band tried to play a Garth Brooks hit. Dickie should be back by now, Maggie thought. John had probably called her from the airport. He would be angry with both of them if he found out they had left the house.

The door burst open, and sunlight spilled into the place. Everyone blinked. Toot barged in, took one look at Maggie, and started to run. "Wait, I want to talk," she said.

Maggie jumped off the stool and reached Toot before he could escape. She grabbed his arm.

"I don't think you've committed a crime," she said. "I'm sorry if I led Hammond to believe you did."

Maggie and Toot sat down at a table away from the bar. The customers stared at them. Toot cleared his throat and began to babble.

"I truly didn't mean to scare you. I just want my name cleared. You don't know how much it means to me. It's all your fault, you know. I ain't never done nothing except be born in this hell hole. People like you think this place is paradise. I never got no money. There are no real jobs here. Most days, I don't got the money for a ferry ticket to get out of here. You high and mighty people throw enough away every year to feed us for a long time. This ain't no beautiful island. It's damn ugly."

"I didn't realize," Maggie said softly, looking into his angry eyes.

"You damn right you didn't, living in that big house behind a guarded gate. Don't even know we're starving over here. Eating dirt. Development's a bad word for you. It may be the only chance we got to make a better living."

"Oh, Toot, I'll get your name cleared for you. I'll talk to Hammond and get it all straight."

"You'd do that for me?" The anger left Toot's eyes. "You may be as nice as Dickie says. Will you talk to my Granny Jones, too? She's very worried about me."

"Of course. Listen, you can help me clear up this matter. I want you to give me information about people on the island. Be eyes and ears for me. You probably know everything that's happening around here. Deal?"

"Whoop-pe-do. It's a deal. I'll go tell my mama you gonna help me."

Toot headed out the door and down the road toward his mama's house.

"Ain't never seen Toot move that fast," Sally Joe commented. "You tell him he done won the sweepstakes?"

"He and I formed a partnership. He's working for me," Maggie said.

"Workin'? Toot? That's a good one," Little Lavender said. "You want another beer? Dickie sent Sister Louis over to tell you he'll be along in a while. He's gone to the ferry dock to pick up our order."

The band had given up on its quest to learn new songs, and some-one had turned up the radio. Patsy Cline was singing about walking the streets after midnight.

Maggie fidgeted on her bar stool. She felt she was wasting pre-cious time. She wished that she'd brought her own car. She didn't need a baby sitter. She wanted to go back to the murder scene and continue her investigation. She felt so close to finding a major clue.

"You gonna help us with our Beach Float party?" Sally Jo asked.

"Spring tide celebration," Maggie answered. "It could be a major fundraiser. Dickie can use the money to paint this place. And maybe find another worthy cause to support. That way the main-landers would want to buy tickets. Sure, I'll help you plan it. Charge five dollars a head. Get some fliers printed and hand them out on the mainland. Get some of these people to help. Sell beer and snacks. What do you think?"

"That you're a genius. Let's do it. We ain't got much time, but we can try."

"It may be small this year, but it could grow. I'll help as much as I can, but I've got other fish to fry."

"No, we ain't having fried fish. Too much trouble to do on the beach," Little Lavender said.

"I meant…oh, never, mind," Maggie said. "Here's some seed money to get us started."

"Pappy told me money don't grow on trees. Reckon he knew it was started as seeds. I guess I done heard it all," Little Lavender chuckled.

Sally Jo tucked the money in her blouse, licked the tip of a pencil she found by the cash register, and started making a to-do list on a napkin.

"Can anybody here give me a ride back to my house? I didn't realize that it would take Dickie so long to get back."

"You can't leave," Sally Jo protested. "We just started our plans. How much beer you think we gotta order? I don't know if we can get that much credit from Lowcountry Beverage Company. Dickie'll be back soon. You can eat supper with us. Mama's frying squirrel that Terrance shot this morning. And squash and beans from the co-op. You ain't never had such good eating."

"I'm really not hungry now. Maybe I'll just have another beer."

Maggie squirmed on her stool wondering how she was ever going to get away from these newfound friends. The sound of a motor pulling into the parking lot answered her question.

Eighteen

"I should have known Dickie would bring you to this garbage dump," S.J. Styles said, earning resentful glances from Sally Jo, Little Lavender, and customers who were close enough to hear her over Patsy Cline's lament about lost love. "I've been all over this island looking for you. You never called me. John told me you were with Dickie."

She stood over Maggie with hands on her hips, eyes blazing.

"Come on, now," she said. "We'll have a quiet dinner at my house. You can fill me in and call John from there. I should have known that scumbag would dump you at his bar. John shouldn't let you run around with this kind of people."

"We're planning a fundraiser. Wanna give a donation for the cause?" Sally Jo asked with surprising meekness. S.J. ignored the question, grabbed Maggie by the arm, and headed toward the door.

These folks seemed to have a resentful respect for S.J.

Settled in the plush leather seat of S.J.'s hunter green Jaguar, Maggie breathed a comfortable sigh. "It's been a long week," she said.

"You certainly chose the wrong time to visit our island. When John told me about your attacks, I was mortified. And Alice. Poor Alice. I'm sure John's devastated."

Maggie didn't bother to reply. Her head hurt from beer on an empty stomach and loud music. She knew she'd be unable to endure the rest of the afternoon and evening with S.J. She'd just make a polite excuse. She'd need to check on Possum. That would be her reason to leave S.J. No one would hurt her in a house with new deadbolt locks on the doors. She felt her pockets for the new keys, then remembered she'd put them in the white pants this morning at the inn.

"What's the matter?" S.J. asked.

"I'm locked out. The new house keys are in my dirty white pants. No, wait. I left those pants to dry on the deck. I may have to throw them away. Anyway, the keys are in the pocket. I'll check as soon as we get there. I'd really like to take a nap. I hope you don't mind if I relax at my place for a while. We can discuss dinner later. I need to check on Possum, too."

"Suit yourself. I just told John that I'd keep an eye on you. I'll be next door." S.J. glanced over at Maggie. "I've been dying to talk to you. I want to hear all about these attacks. What's your theory on these murders? Hammond told me you keep getting in his way."

"He can't be serious. I think he's forgetting that I'm the victim of those attacks."

"You're safe now. I'll let you recharge and we'll make plans later."

The Jag sped through the security gate. S.J. didn't bother to slow down. The oval pass on the windshield gave her a privilege that Toot and Dickie would never have. Since they were almost at the beach house, Maggie decided to pump S.J. for a little information.

"Have you known Robert Davis for a long time?" she asked.

"Such a nice man. He's giving money to our art program. I met him a few months ago. Why?"

"I think he's involved with Joe and the 'gator poachers. Hammond is checking to see if he owns the boat they've been using."

S.J. waved the notion away. "Absurd. I can see why Hammond thinks you're sticking your nose in where it doesn't belong. Robert is a gentleman. Alice and I both thought so."

S.J. pulled the car into the Meyers' driveway. Maggie opened the door and almost got out without a word. Then she remembered something she had meant to ask S.J. "I need the guest list from your party. Someone at the party took my door keys."

144

"Everyone who's anyone on this island attended my party. And they don't steal. They can buy whatever they want. You rest now. Your head will clear after a nap. The pollution from that horrid bar has warped your senses."

S.J. started the car. Maggie closed the door without responding. Rather than looking S.J. in the eye, Maggie glanced at the back seat. A large box with red satin ribbon spilling out occupied the floor.

"Wait," Maggie called. "Where'd you get the ribbon?"

"Ribbon? Oh, the ribbon," S.J. said. "At the Mainland Fire Department, like everyone else."

The car spun around in the street and S.J. headed back toward the gate, not next door to her house.

Maggie walked around the house to the deck. S.J. didn't even bother to stay around and make sure she wasn't locked out. Great, Maggie thought. The white pants weren't where she left them. She was looking for them when she heard the phone ring inside the house. She hurried up the steps. The back door was wide open. Without thinking, she bolted through the door and grabbed the phone on the fourth ring.

"Thank God, you're there," she heard John say. "Did you and Dickie take a walk on the beach?"

Maggie explained the previous events ending with S.J.'s rude and abrupt departure. John laughed. "S.J.'s always been that way. Wants everyone to think she's the temperamental artist."

"I've lost my new keys. They were in those dirty white pants I wore this morning. I think the pants blew off the deck. We've got a stiff wind this afternoon. I was in the bushes looking for them when you called, and I ran in to get the phone." A chill crept up Maggie's spine when she realized what had happened.

"John, the door to the house, the deck door, was standing open. Do you think Dickie forgot to close it when he dropped me at the Red-Eye?"

"Dickie would forget his truck if he wasn't riding in it, and you lose more keys than anyone I've ever met," John said with affectionate amusement in his voice.

"Do you lose fabric swatches like you lose keys? If we find your keys, shall we have them made into earrings and fasten them to your ears?"

"This is no laughing matter. I guess Possum and I'll go back for another night at the inn."

"Not on your life. I want you in a safer place until Ken Hammond makes his arrests, and I don't want you alone."

"That could take years."

"Maude and I have decided that you're to be our guest, at my house, until your vacation is over. Maude wants someone to look after while I'm gone. She'll love Possum."

"Gone? I thought you'd be back for the party Saturday."

"I will. Ralph wants me to go from Connecticut to Long Island for Alice's funeral. I'll be back Saturday afternoon. We'll go to the Beach Float at Liberty Oak together. In the meantime, you'll stay at my house. Take the main road past the Liberty Oak turnoff. Three miles and then a right down my driveway. Maude's waiting for you."

A note of tenderness crept into his voice. "I want you to be safe while I'm gone."

"I'm too exhausted to argue. I'll stay at your house. I'll be there as soon as I pack and close up this place."

In less than an hour, Maggie had packed her car and stowed Possum, with food and toys, on the back seat. They headed for the Heywards'. As she turned into the driveway, she realized that the Elliot Inn looked shabby compared to the Heyward plantation. Maude stood on the top step as Maggie stopped the Volvo in front of a four-column front piazza that wound around a massive, white, three-story structure. Soft pink azaleas flanked the house, and gleaming polished brass twinkled from the front door knocker.

"Welcome, Miss Maggie. Clarence, come on and take these bags upstairs to the second floor front guest room. Miss Maggie, you're to have a guest room with a view of our ocean. I'll look after you good. We never had this much trouble on Seaward since I been working here. And that's since the day I was born. Just terrible."

Maggie followed Maude and Clarence into the entrance hall and up wide, curving steps to the second floor.

Clarence gripped the handle of Possum's pet taxi. "This dog is gonna grow out of this cage in no time," he said. "She sure is beautiful." He opened the cage after he'd carefully set the kennel on the bedroom floor. Possum came bounding out and headed straight for Maggie's sandals. She tried to chew on the strap. Maggie picked her up and cuddled the squirming puppy.

Maude had been talking since they'd entered the room.

"We can't even tell Mrs. Heyward about Alice. She never got over the death of Miss Catherine. Tragic, just tragic."

Maggie couldn't decide if she meant Alice's death or Catherine's. She did remember that John had told her Alice was on the boat when Catherine drowned.

"Hope you like your quarters. This is the very room where mainland Confederates met before they went off to kill them damn Yankees," Maude said with a chuckle.

"I'll be sleeping in a room filled with history. It's almost like a museum. But not stuffy." Maggie admired the Battenberg lace coverlet on the four-poster rice bed. An eighteenth century mahogany secretary stood opposite the bed. Family pictures filled the shelves behind the glass. A picture of John when he was a child seemed to be the focal point of the display. Maggie looked closely.

"He was adorable, even when he was a boy," she said.

"He was a little hellion," Maude replied with pride in her voice. "Here's your bags. You get settled in, and we'll have dinner ready soon. Ain't nobody can get you now. We only got friendly ghosts here."

Maude and Clarence withdrew and closed the door, and Maggie flopped across the bed. Possum curled into the crook of her arm. This would be a good time to review the events of the week. Maggie felt that she'd missed something somewhere. The key to this puzzle seemed to be a piece of information that the killer thought Maggie knew.

The key, she thought, and her mind made a hopeful leap. Losing her new keys had brought her to John's house. Was he merely offering her Southern hospitality or was this the beginning of a real relationship? Maggie turned over on her stomach and pounded the pillow with her fist. She would be in Rosemont, and he lived here, unless she decided to move to Atlanta and join the Chandler Design firm. Take it as it comes, she thought, and turned her mind back to Michael's murder.

Possum jumped on her head and tried to bite Maggie's hair with her sharp puppy teeth. She grabbed Possum and settled the dog next to her.

Hammond seemed incompetent. If she found the answer, would he believe her? She needed to prove that Michael had stumbled on the poachers and had been silenced forever. A similar situation must have occurred with Alice. Robert Davis had probably made the phone call to Alice. She'd admitted that, because of her newspaper gossip column, she knew everyone and everything on Seaward. If Hammond proved that Davis owned the boat and Joe had been driving it and Alice found out...

Maggie's ruminating was interrupted by a soft tap on the bedroom door. "Miss Maggie, supper's ready," Maude called. "You want to eat in the dining room or share the kitchen table with me and Clarence?"

Maggie opened the door and smiled at Maude. "Kitchen, of course. I want to be treated like one of the family. I'll take Possum out to tend to her business and be right there."

A hearty meal awaited Maggie at the kitchen table. Three places had been set. Evidently, John had told Maude that Maggie was more than a guest. Maggie settled herself at the table and put a soft blue linen napkin in her lap. Possum curled beside the sturdy pine chair and emitted a contented puppy sigh.

"I made my special deviled crab for you. It's one of John's favorite dishes. Clarence cleaned the crabs this afternoon. I made sweet potato pie, too. You thin enough to eat two pieces."

"Tell me about your Confederate ghosts," Maggie said. "There must be a legend connected with this place."

"Lots of 'em, honey," Clarence said, as he bit into a moist and fluffy buttermilk biscuit.

"You ain't scaring this lady with no ghost tales tonight," Maude said. "She's with us 'til they catch that awful killer."

"Aw, Maude, I was just gonna tell her about during the war they buried the silver out in the rice fields. The tide washed it away before the Heywards could reclaim it. It's probably still floating somewhere in the Atlantic Ocean."

"That could be it!" Maggie shouted, causing her companions to jump in their seats.

"What?" Maude and Clarence said together.

"The tide. The tide washed away an important clue from the murder scene. That's why I haven't been able to make any sense out of it," Maggie answered. "Joe said something about the tide would change soon. The killer probably knew that the tide would wash the clues away. Probably thought the body would be gone, too. That's why he was surprised when I found it."

149

Maude and Clarence looked at each other. Nothing made sense to them. Then the phone rang, and Maggie stopped theorizing.

"It's for you, Miss Maggie. Mister Heyward's calling from way up North."

Clarence handed the portable phone to Maggie and disappeared into the pantry with Maude.

"The Heyward Plantation is magnificent," Maggie told John. "Thank you for inviting me over. This is the perfect way to spend the rest of my vacation."

"I called because I forgot to tell you Dickie and the gang want you to meet with them at the inn in the morning at eleven. Billy's got a radio D.J. and wants you to talk to him. You certainly got those bums stirred up."

"I thought you called to say you missed me."

"That, too."

"John, do you happen to remember what you said to S.J. about my attacks? She was so snooty about it. I don't want her passing on rumors that aren't true."

"I don't remember telling her anything, but so much has happened, it's hard to keep track. I gotta go. Ralph's calling for me. We'll discuss this when I get back. Take care. And I do miss you."

"Me, too," Maggie answered.

She wandered back to the kitchen, ready for sweet potato pie. But Maude interrupted her before she could take a bite.

"You're popular tonight. Deputy Watson's waiting for you at the back door. Sent me to get you. Says he's in a hurry, but he promised Hammond he'd make sure you were safe. Wants to let you know the news."

"What news?"

"They found that security guard, Joe, up near Orangeburg in Robert Davis' truck. A whole pile of 'gator hides was a-riding in the back of that truck."

Nineteen

Maggie stretched her legs and settled into the creaky old wooden rocker on Granny Jones' porch. She felt a soothing peace for the first time since arriving on Seaward. Last night, in the Heywards' antique rice bed, had been the first sleep without nightmares since she'd arrived on Seaward. Even Possum liked the fresh sea breezes blowing through the window screens. Tree frogs croaked a steady rhythm, and the morning light danced on the counterpane to give Maggie and Possum a gentle wake-up call.

She decided to leave Possum with Clarence. Maggie had errands to run and didn't want to leave Possum in her hot car. Before going back to the murder scene, which she could accomplish without anyone's knowledge, she decided to check the inn and find out if Sally Jo and Little Lavender had actually assembled anyone to get the beach party under way. She'd been thinking that sending some of the island children to camp on the mainland could be a worthy cause for the fundraiser. More people would be willing to buy tickets. Maybe a scholarship program could be started in order to give all island children a chance to experience a summer change of environment.

Maggie swayed back and forth in the old rocker. A visit to the old lady's house had been a last-minute decision. She'd remembered that she'd promised Dickie she'd go see Toot's grandmother. She owed it to Toot Sweet to put in a good word for him with his relatives. Granny Jones was the oldest living member of the original settlers on Seaward. Her knowledge of herbs and potions for human ailments gave her the reigning status of island mentor. It had been a wonderful morning. Maggie could listen forever to the tales that Granny Jones told as she dipped snuff in a very lady-like manner.

"We tell time around here by the rise and fall of the tides," Granny Jones stated. "The water marks the passing hours and seasons, too. Human comings and goings be the same way. It all be the same on Seaward Island."

Granny Jones' doublewide mobile home was hidden behind wild magnolias on the edge of a cypress swamp. Her family's wooden structure had burned during a wind shift on garbage burning day. Granny's home of recent years had been purchased and given to her by the Heywards. Maggie suspected her colleagues in the Rosemont Design Firm wouldn't believe it: Strings of Christmas lights outlined the edge of the structure. Wild flowers and herbs grew profusely in front of the mobile home. A solitary crane stood near the bank of the swamp. Particles of sunlight filtered through the live oak trees that were heavily draped with Spanish moss.

"I hope you realize I meant no harm to Toot. I'm sure he was just frightened. I'm going to do everything I can to make it right with him and Sheriff Hammond."

"You'd do better to sweep before your own door, young lady," Granny Jones replied. "Don't need no mainland people messing in our affairs. Toot's always been able to take care of hisself. It's time for me to do my daily Bible studying. Mr. Heyward is learning me to read. Imagine that, at my age. I promised Dickie I'd send him some flea powder. You take it to him for me?"

"Flea powder? For him or his dogs?"

Granny ignored the comment and kept talking. "Garlic powder and brewers powdered yeast mixed together. Put it on their food every day. Them fleas'll be gone in a couple of months. We still do things the best way around these parts. Might do them mainlanders some good to take a lesson from us. When we use our resources, we replenish what we use. We don't throw away just 'cause something gets dirty."

"Good advice, Granny." Maggie thought about the white pants she'd planned to throw away.

"One more thing, child. You'll be happy if you got something interesting to do, somebody to love, and something to look forward to."

"Right now I'm late for the fundraising meeting. I'm not sure that I should look forward to that."

"Don't underestimate island folks. They getting together the best time you'll ever have. Just beware of the mean reds."

"What? Watch out for what?"

Granny slammed the screen door and disappeared inside. Maggie turned and walked toward her car, clutching the vial of flea powder. Did she say 'mean red'? Did that refer to ribbons? Ridiculous. Granny didn't know what she was talking about. Or did she?

Although she was perturbed by Granny's ominous warning, by the time Maggie arrived at the inn, she was ready to deal with the chaos in the little room behind the inn's kitchen. Everyone was shouting and not listening to each other as Maggie settled herself at the head of the table.

"It's time to call this meeting to order," she said.

Several snickers and giggles floated through the air. Maggie looked around. At least a dozen people had come. Interest was running high. The regulars from the Red-Eye wanted to get in on the action.

"Sally Jo, if you have your list, we'll start there. There's not much we can do in this short time. It takes months and months to plan a successful fundraiser. The one I did in Rosemont for a local theater group took six months. Don't be disappointed if you only make a few dollars."

The group stared at Maggie as if she had two heads and was speaking in a foreign language. Determined not to get exasperated, she forged ahead.

153

"Read the list and tell me what's been done."

Maggie groaned inwardly and tried to listen to Sally Jo and the gang talk about their plans. It would be impossible to pull this together. At least it was giving the bar regulars a focus. If they accomplished a third of their plans, they wouldn't have time to sit around the bar and drink all day. Billy, the night clerk at the inn, would print tickets on their copy machine.

"Order, order." Maggie banged on the table with a plastic water cup. "Let's give the mainlanders an incentive to buy these tickets. I'll donate two days and nights in the honeymoon suite. Number each ticket. We'll draw for the prize at the end of the evening. You have to be there to win. That should sell a few tickets. Someone ask the Kash and Karry if they'll give a certificate for some free groceries. And check the tennis club. Maybe they'll donate a prize."

"You're a genius, a real genius. How you know about these things?" Sally Jo asked. She was scribbling these suggestions on the back of her soiled napkin.

"I've been affiliated with volunteer work in Rosemont. There are times that I'd like to hang up my pearls, but giving time and effort to your community raises the standard of living and promotes a better way of life for its people," Maggie answered.

The group, once more, looked at Maggie as if she were crazy.

"We always just help each other," Sally Jo said. "We never look for help from outsiders."

"Go out and get started," Maggie said. "If you run into a problem, call me at Mister Heyward's house. I'll be there the rest of the week. Let's meet back at the Red-Eye this afternoon at five o'clock. We'll see how much we've accomplished."

The group looked at Maggie as if she'd just announced that the *Queen Elizabeth II* had docked at Markley's Landing.

"Go on now. You can do it. Mister Heyward is at Alice's funeral. I'm helping Maude with things that needed to be done."

154

More giggles from the group.

Maggie wanted to kick herself for offering an explanation of her private life to strangers. Something about John made her lose control. It felt good to say his name out loud. She smiled to herself.

After settling with the inn on a prize for the fundraiser, Maggie slid into the warm leather seat of the Volvo and headed the car toward the lagoon. Finally, it was time for her to start back at square one and try to piece together a plausible solution to the murder. Dickie and John would never have to know she'd gone alone.

Maggie parked the car across from the security gate and headed toward the trail to the lagoon. The guard chattered into the phone and didn't see her disappear into the quiet of the swamp, a wonderful respite after the noise and confusion of those island rowdies.

Suddenly, Maggie halted in her tracks. Before her lay a scene she had witnessed at S.J.'s house. The murder scene. Who came here every day to paint? The murderer? Michael? The poachers would not have been out at this time of day. The light and shadows matched the canvas. The killer had been waiting. He had picked up the driftwood and beat a defenseless Michael to death. Michael knew his killer.

Maggie felt the weight of an arm on her shoulder. She screamed.

"What are you doing here alone?" Robert Davis asked.

Maggie jumped and pulled away. "I thought you were in jail," she said.

"Jail? For what?"

"Poaching 'gators. The highway patrol caught Joe in your truck. Did you escape?" Maggie inched away from Robert while they were talking. He took a step toward her.

"Escape? Oh, I see. You think I'm one of the poachers," Robert laughed. He backed away from Maggie. "I've been on the mainland for the last two days attending Chamber of Commerce meetings. The Mainland Chamber wants me to invest in that old island marina. Start growth on the island again. Joe stole my truck. I had it parked near the mainland dock. Use it when I go over. I can't believe you thought I was part of that crowd," Robert added, chuckling.

Although she was still weak in the knees, Maggie felt a bit of courage returning. Hopefully, this man was telling the truth.

"If you have nothing to do with this, then why are you here at the murder scene?"

"Murder scene? I'm taking my afternoon walk, like I do every afternoon when I'm on the island. I didn't even know this was where the boy got killed. What are you doing here?"

"Taking a walk, too," Maggie replied.

Ken Hammond came crashing down the trail, breathless.

"I heard a scream. I was on my way to the Meyers' house. Gonna get prints off the door. What the hell is going on?" Hammond said.

"All my suspects have alibis," Maggie calmly replied. "Do yours?"

"I shoulda known it was you. Running around this island all week getting the place in an uproar. I just caught Little Lavender at the Kash and Karry trying to con Mrs. Templeman into giving him a month's worth of groceries. You gonna have the whole island out begging. Won't get another lick of work out of 'em."

"I'll talk to Mrs. Templeman. When she understands what we're doing, she'll be happy to donate," Maggie said.

"Let me do it," Robert said. "I heard what you're trying to do and think it's a great idea. Sorry I scared you. I can't believe you thought I was a bad guy. I'll go over to the store right now."

Hammond watched Davis leave and then turned to Maggie. "That man's worth millions. You thought he was a killer? What other wacky theories you been working on?"

"What about Joe and the 'gator poachers?"

"Guilty, but not of murder. Joe came on duty ten minutes before you found the body. He'd been on the mainland all day making plans with his cohorts to move the 'gator hides. At least six people rode over with him on the *Mary Grace* that afternoon. Any more ideas from your corner of the design world? Have you thought up any new designs that might just make sense, little lady?"

"One of our suspects is lying. And don't call me 'little lady'. I'm Maggie to friends. Margaret to you."

"Don't tell me how to do my job. Seems that's what you been doing all week. Are you going home soon?"

"I'm a guest of Mister Heyward. I don't know how long it'll be. If I stay until you catch the killer, I could become a permanent resident."

The sheriff's face turned bright red, whether out of embarrassment or anger, Maggie couldn't say.

"Stay out of my way," he snarled. "I'll arrest you for interfering with the law. The next time you cry wolf, you better make it loud enough for the mainland police to hear. I got better things to do."

Maggie watched him stomp away. She knew he was furious that she'd found the poachers' boat and he'd been working on it for months. Sometimes a fresh perspective made a difference. She was standing in the swamp and couldn't see the water. Like the forest and the trees. She'd concentrate on the fundraiser and hope she'd regain that perspective.

Turning to leave, she glanced back and watched an alligator on the opposite bank slither into the water and glide down the waterway.

"At least you're safe now," she said.

Twenty

" Amazing. Simply amazing," Maggie said.

Dickie, Maggie, and Robert Davis were standing on the bank near the Liberty Oak. After Maggie had checked on Possum and declared Clarence the best dog sitter of all time, she hurried out to the fundraising scene. Robert had stepped in and organized the band of Red-Eye regulars. Dickie had put the final string of white lights on the proud old oak.

The Seaward Inn had donated its small power generator. Dickie flipped the switch and the tree came to life.

"Beautiful. Like a fairy land," Robert said. "It'll be outstanding tonight."

Maggie looked around. Even the banner donated by the Lowcountry Beverage Company waved smartly in the breeze. It was a generic ad for their beer, but it added a festive touch for the occasion. Next year, the company would have time to print "Beach Float at Liberty Oak." The rag-tag Red-Eye regulars wanted to continue their efforts to improve the standard of living on the island without outside interference.

Maggie and Robert shook hands. Their combined force and leadership had made this happen. If they only knew how many tickets had been sold. Everyone was reporting a different number. Three or four hundred. It was anybody's guess. Terrance claimed he'd sold fifty outside of Aunt Patty's Cafe. No one had seen the money for those tickets. Sally Jo had spent the afternoon making a pink neon halter top from a pattern her mama had bought at the Lowland Flea Market. Her tickets were still sitting on the sewing machine. She claimed she needed something new to wear to sell tickets on the mainland. This fundraiser was a surprise party. It would be a surprise to see how many people came, Maggie thought.

"S.J. and I are coming together," Robert said. "I talked her into getting out. She's so upset about Michael and Alice. Tragic. You and John are coming too, I suppose."

"He'll be back by four this afternoon if his plane's on time. He told me to come without him and he'd meet me here."

"Gotta go. The barbecue's coming on the next run of the *Mary Grace*. I still think three dollars a plate's too cheap. But I guess it's all this bunch can afford. You and Dickie recheck your list. We'll re-group by phone to smooth the rough edges of this affair," Robert said.

Maggie and Dickie waved as he left.

"I got my car," Toot Sweet hollered as he came down the path like a banshee chasing wild pigs in the woods. "Hammond give it back." Toot grabbed Maggie and gave her a big wet smack on the cheek.

"Hammond? I gave Granny Jones the money to pay Hammond for your bail. How did Hammond get your car?" Maggie asked.

"He always had it."

"Wait a minute," Dickie said, "this don't sound right. What'd he tell you?"

"He told Mama he'd impounded it for my bail. First, he told her he'd sold it. Mama just told me the car'd been sold to make my bail. I was so upset, I didn't ask her who. Until you made your deal with me. Don't matter. I give him the money. He give me the car. Now I can help you. What you want me to do?"

Maggie and Dickie looked at each other. "You know what this means," Dickie said.

"When we were shot at, at the old marina, Hammond had Toot's car. Come on. Let's go talk to him," Maggie said, turning to go.

"Whoa," Dickie said. "We can't just run up to him and accuse him of shooting at us."

"You're right. We need to think this through. If Hammond's the killer, it would explain everything. And Watson's my attacker. The day Watson came over, he seemed right at home. He and Hammond have discouraged me. We'll set a trap for them at the Beach Float. Robert has asked for volunteers from the Mainland Police Department to come over and help us with crowd control. We'll have their protection. Toot, here's how you can help."

The three sat under the Liberty Oak as Dickie and Maggie formulated a plan to get the murderer to attack Maggie again, but this time, Dickie would be there to protect her. He would sound the alarm, and the mainland police would come charging in.

Toot couldn't quite follow their logic. "All I heard is somebody in my Caddy shot at you. Does that mean they was going around trying to kill everybody on the island, and just got Michael and Alice?"

"No, Toot, I mean we've got to have more proof to pin on Hammond. We need to have a motive," Maggie answered.

"Easy," Dickie said. "Michael and Alice caught Hammond covering for the alligator poachers and threatened to turn him in. Hammond's been sheriff so long, he'd be disgraced. And go to jail, too. Boy, would I love to see that, the way he's always after us at the Red-Eye."

Toot watched Maggie and Dickie talking, his head snapping from side to side as he watched each one speak and tried to understand what they were talking about. Maggie thought he looked a little like he was trying to keep up with the ball at a tennis match. Finally, he interrupted. "I'm hungry," he said. "I ain't had breakfast and it's past lunchtime."

"Okay, Toot," Maggie said, "you go get something to eat. Remember what you're supposed to do tonight. Dickie and I are going over to Tom Murphy's. I saw red ribbon at their house the day John

161

and I were marooned in the storm. I need to see if they know how it fits."

Dickie looked doubtful, but he agreed to go along.

"This seems pretty far-fetched," he said as he drove toward the Murphys' place. "You want us to get that ribbon you saw at the Murphys' and have it tested for fingerprints? What's that gonna prove?"

"Maybe nothing. We can at least ask the Murphys where they got the ribbon. Have you had chicken pox? The Murphy kids have a rampant case."

"On Seaward, we probably had everything known to man. Some folks still eat vegetables to prevent scurvy."

"Which reminds me," Maggie said, "I want to buy some fresh vegetables from the co-op before I go home. Maude had melt-in-your-mouth sliced tomatoes at dinner last night. If I lived here, I'd gain twenty pounds a week."

The pickup truck bounced down the gravel road into the Murphys' yard. The front door swung open and children spilled into the yard. Mandy had a red satin bow in her hair.

"Where did you get the pretty bow in your hair?" Maggie asked. To keep from jerking the ribbon out of the child's hair, she clutched her hands together.

"My school gave everybody one. We're supposed to wear it on our blouses. Tells everybody we're drug-free. I like mine better in my hair. When mama gives me Tylenol for my chicken pox, is that a drug?"

"The good kind," Maggie answered. "It makes you better, not sick." She hoped she was giving the right advice to the child. She hid her disappointment that Hammond hadn't left the red ribbon at the Murphys'.

"Come in," Julie called out. "Where's John? I've been making brownies for two days for the Beach Float. Hope we won't be rained out."

"John's not back from Long Island. He'll be in late this afternoon. Dickie and I were just riding by and thought we'd stop and see if you were coming with the children or if we should take your brownies for you."

"How kind of you. The doctor says the worst is over. We went to the mainland yesterday for a recheck. No one is contagious. Hope you didn't get it."

"Me, too. The doctor says for adults it's shingles and really serious. Well, see you tonight."

Maggie and Dickie climbed back in the truck. They both knew this had been a waste of time.

"I don't know what to do next, Dickie."

"If our plan doesn't work tonight, we'll tell the mainland police everything we know; let them investigate Hammond."

"I guess we'll have to. I don't know what else to do."

They sat silently until the truck pulled into the Heywards' driveway.

"Thanks, Dickie. I'll see you tonight. Hope we get enough money to paint the Red-Eye and send some island children to a nice summer camp.

"Thank you for going to see Granny Jones. She'd heard so much about you, she was busting a gut to get to meet you."

"She certainly didn't act like it," Maggie said. "She gave me a scary warning about the mean reds. I haven't figured out what she meant."

Dickie laughed so hard, he almost fell out of the truck.

"She says that to everybody she likes. Can't believe you thought she was a-warning you."

"Why does she say that to everyone?"

"About twenty years ago, Granny Jones left the island and went to a movie, only one she ever seen at a theater. It was about some woman who got depressed and ate breakfast in front of some jewelry store. Don't make sense to me, but anyhow, Granny claimed that when this woman was unhappy she had a bad case of the mean reds. By saying to watch out for the mean reds she was a telling you to stay happy."

" 'Breakfast at Tiffany's'. That was one of my favorite movies when I was a little girl. You know, Dickie, that's the way my whole week of vacation has been. I have misinterpreted and misunderstood the clues to Michael's murder. That's what Hammond was counting on. Call if anything happens. I'll see you tonight."

Maggie walked slowly into the house and followed the smell of boiled, fresh shrimp into the kitchen.

"John's gonna be late," Maude said. "Mister Randolph collapsed at the funeral and John's gonna take a later flight. Hope he'll be here before we're done with the party. Robert Davis called, too. He says everything is ready for the mob, and you just need to show up."

"Maude, oh, Maude, I've got a case of the mean reds."

"You breaking out with chicken pox already?"

"Not yet. I wish it were that easy. I've just misinterpreted clues and haven't had enough to go on. Sheriff Hammond kept so much from me. I want to start at the beginning. Will you listen while I talk my way through this?"

"If you help me peel these shrimps. I promised John I'd cook my famous Shrimp Creole for you tomorrow. You can eat a few while we do this. I boiled a plenty. Clarence took Possum down to the creek. He says you shore got a smart puppy. Already trained that dog to sit."

By the time the shrimp shells flowed in mounds over the bowls, Maggie had talked her way through the events of the entire week.

164

"Simple, Maude. Dickie and I have a plan, but I wish I could talk to him. That's the first thing he's doing with his fundraising money, a new telephone at the Red-Eye. I'm taking a shower and decking out in my perfect party dress. This will be an evening to remember."

Twenty-one

The Volvo crept slowly down the main road. People lined the highway, and they were all heading toward the beach and the Liberty Oak. Not a space within a mile to park the Volvo. The avenue to the oak was jammed with more people. A catastrophe had occurred. The power generator must have blown. Had anyone been hurt? That would be the only reason this many people had converged.

"Maggie, Maggie," Dickie called, "park that car and get down here now. Everything's set for our plan. Where you been?"

Maggie pulled off the road into the soft sand, hopped out, locked the door, and ran toward Dickie.

"What's wrong? Is anybody hurt?"

"Not yet. But tempers'll flare if we don't have enough food for these people. At five dollars a head, we're rich. You're wonderful, Maggie, wonderful."

"Nothing awful's happened? All these people came for the Beach Float?"

"Having a ball, too. Nobody can believe the success we got here. All because of you. You believed in us. The *Mary Grace* is making another run, bringing a keg this time and more people. Where's John?"

"Maybe he'll be on the next ferry run. He caught a later flight from New York," Maggie answered.

They came to the end of the road and looked at the sea of revelers enjoying the first, and maybe annual, Beach Float at Liberty Oak. One group played beach volleyball; another tried to limbo to the impossible tempo of the Red-Eye Quartet. Maggie smiled. The D.J., Tuffy Surf from ZQ-106, grabbed the microphone and began the first live remote broadcast from Seaward Island.

167

Maggie began to drift through the crowd looking for familiar faces. She saw Toot perched on a blanket with three girls. Robert Davis stood behind a counter slinging hash. His broad grin showed how delighted he was with their efforts.

"You and John are doing the ten-to-midnight shift," he hollered above the noise of a long line in front of the stand.

"Sounds good to me," Maggie replied.

There couldn't be that many hungry people late in the evening. Young couples with their children were finishing their dinner. Maggie waved to Tom Murphy and his clan. She wished that John would arrive. Then the party would be as much fun for her as it was for these people.

She walked beyond the crowd. Time to put the plan into action. She looked around and caught Dickie's eye. He waved. That was his go-ahead sign, she decided.

Dark was falling. The evening star twinkled in the dusk, and Maggie kept walking down the beach, away from the crowd. To lure her attacker, she needed to be away from the noise and gaiety. She hoped enough people had seen her wander away. She also hoped that Dickie wasn't far behind her, but was well hidden. She looked around. Everything looked normal. A heron screeched in the bushes.

Ahead, Maggie saw a huge lump in the sand. While waiting for something to happen, she decided to investigate. As she drew near, the lump began to move. The biggest turtle Maggie had ever seen struggled to crawl back to the ocean. The rough outer shell was actually large enough for Maggie to sit on. But she didn't. She hunched down to take a closer look. The turtle stared straight ahead and kept inching its way to the sea. Turtle eggs were hidden in a nest behind the dunes. The spring tide had brought the turtles back to Seaward.

As Maggie looked from the turtle to the sky, a shadow passed over her. A rough, black cloth scratched her chin. The attacker had taken their bait! Dickie would jump out of sea oats with a surprise ambush. Maggie drew a deep breath and waited. Nothing happened.

Maggie tried to call his name, but her voice was muffled by the burlap cloth and the roar of the spring tide crashing and pounding on the beach.

Rough, damp rope went around Maggie's ankles and secured her legs together. She wasn't able to move. She realized, too late, that she must fight back. She tried to scream. Her arms thrashed against the burlap. The bag was pulled over her body and she felt hands pushing against her weak resistance. She was rolling over and over toward the ocean. Shells punctured the cloth and bit into her sides. A watery grave. The nightmare was happening. Maggie took a deep breath. The rolling stopped. The ocean receded and Maggie knew that she was being dumped like a sack of potatoes onto the floorboard of a car. What was happening? It was all too fast. Where was Dickie? It wasn't supposed to be this way. When the attacker grabbed her, Dickie was supposed to sneak up from behind and hit him, and then call for help. Instead, Maggie felt each blow that carried her into darkness.

Twenty-two

"Where's Maggie?" John asked. "I can't believe the turnout for this. The *Mary Grace* was packed when I came over. Beach Float is a moneymaker."

"Fantastic, ain't it?" Dickie said. "Maggie's around. I had to set up the new keg." Suddenly, he looked at John in alarm, and his face turned pale.

"Oh, God, I was supposed to follow Maggie and help her catch the killer. You don't reckon she went ahead without me?"

John glared at him in disbelief. "What foolishness did you two cook up?"

"You look like it wasn't a swift idea. Let's find Maggie and call it off. You ain't gonna believe her latest scheme."

John began to push through the crowd, straining to catch a glimpse of Maggie's slim figure. Dickie followed closely. He was beginning to be nervous. But surely Maggie wouldn't go without telling him.

Little Lavender charged up in front of them. He was wearing a purple-checked shirt made from tablecloth material.

"Like my new threads?" he asked. "Sally Jo's mama made it last night. Jerked this cloth right off of Jimmy Sue's table. It's tucked in so's you don't see the ketchup spot."

"Shut up and help us find Maggie," Dickie said.

"Is she missing?" Little Lavender asked.

"I can't believe you two," John said angrily to Dickie. "I don't want to know what you were thinking. I just want to find Maggie."

John spotted Robert and called his name. "You seen Maggie?"

"Not for a while. S.J. went home to get a shawl. Thinks it's going to be chilly tonight. Maybe Maggie rode with her. There's Hammond. Ask him," Robert said.

171

Ken Hammond came charging toward the group waving a piece of torn paper. "What the hell is this all about?" he said.

"Maggie thought maybe you was the killer. We's suppose to catch you tonight," Dickie said, keeping his head down and carefully avoiding the sheriff's eyes.

"I'm putting every one of you idiots behind bars. Imagine that Toot trying to write me a note to meet Maggie down by south beach! We finally got prints off one of those ribbons that have been floating around. Where is she?"

"She's done lured the real killer to the meeting spot. I'm s'posed to be there to save her," Dickie said.

"Come on. The fog's rolling in. Hammond, alert everybody. Search for Maggie. Get Tuffy Surf to announce it over his radio system. Let's go toward south beach," John said.

Twenty-three

The hard concrete dug into the cuts and bruises on Maggie's back. It had been at least an hour since her abduction and she was still alive. She knew that she must be in the empty marina building. She drifted in and out of consciousness. Suddenly, she felt a presence standing over her.

"Help. Please, help me," she said. Blood trickled from her lip and oozed into the black covering that prevented escape. The ropes cut into her ankles, and her fingers felt numb. She tried to turn over and slammed herself against the person standing above her. An insistent beep pierced her ears. Eight beeps. None of this made sense, she thought as she drifted in and out of consciousness.

She shook her head and tried to stay awake. She couldn't tell how much time had passed. The beeps had stopped. Maggie knew she'd heard the sound before. Recently. She had to focus. Recognizing the killer would give her a chance. Two more beeps.

Sondra Jean Styles' sun-watch.

"S.J.? You?" Maggie mumbled through the dried blood around her lips.

A foot kicked Maggie with enough force to roll her over on her back. "Please let me out of this wrap. Let's talk. Why did you kill Michael, and why Alice? She was your friend." Maggie had to strain to form the words. The wrap felt like a sticky body bag. Her breathing was shallow.

S.J. untied her ankles, grabbed the black covering, and jerked it above Maggie's head. Her body hit the hard concrete. She curled her body into the fetal position and covered her eyes. Darkness had crept over the island, and the bare light bulbs from dangling fixtures burned Maggie's eyes.

"Okay, bitch. You want to know? You stupid bitch. Flitting around my island, acting like you own Seaward. Getting it on with John Heyward. What the hell do you know about what's good for us?" Spittle ran down S.J.'s chin. Her eyes were dilated and too fixed for the bright lights. Maggie realized S.J. was a drug addict.

"You left the red ribbon beside Michael as a slap in the face to Sheriff Hammond, didn't you?"

S.J. ignored Maggie's pleading question and began to ramble, her voice a monotone.

"When we discussed my sun-watch on the beach, I thought you knew it was Michael's. I took it off his arm after I killed him. He would have turned me in, destroyed my art school. I wouldn't be able to give the students the drugs they needed to be creative. I stole your keys. Broke in. I wanted to know how much you knew. I tried to warn you to stay away. I had to kill him to preserve my school. He was going to tell the authorities about the drugs.

"Alice was a fool," S.J. said. "She pushed Catherine, John's sister, overboard. Jealousy. I was blackmailing her to help fund my art students. When I confided in her about Michael, she threatened to tell Hammond. I shut her up the same way I plan to destroy you. By tomorrow at noon, the tide will have washed your body out to sea."

S.J.'s eyes gleamed with pleasure.

Maggie looked up and tried to focus. A red ribbon dangled loosely from S.J.'s fist.

"I still don't know why the hell you wanted that obnoxious dog that Michael was so crazy for. I had already informed him that if he spent the summer with me, the dog had to go. I would have killed her, too, but she ran. I thought you'd guessed by now the dog belonged to Michael."

"Possum was Michael's dog?" Maggie tried to focus her thoughts. Keep S.J. talking, she thought. Stall for time. Someone at the Beach Float would miss them and come looking.

Twenty-four

John stumbled through the bushes. Not a trace of Maggie.
"Dickie, you see anything?"

"Come here," Dickie answered. "You think these car tracks look
fresh?"

John leaned over and studied the tire marks. "I don't know," he
said. "It's far enough away from the party. Maybe the killer abduc-
ted her here, threw her in a car, and then what?"

"Took her somewhere," Dickie said.

"Damn it, Dickie, I know that, but where?" John said. "Here comes Hammond."

"Watson radioed," the sheriff said. "Says S.J. never went home.
Her prints were all over the ribbon that killed Alice. She's not at the
lagoon or anywhere on the other side of Seaward. She's taken Maggie to some place on this side of the island."

"You're telling me that S.J.'s the killer?" John said. He stared at
Hammond in disbelief.

"Crime of passion is the way I figure it. Then she couldn't live
with it. Told Alice, got scared, and killed her, too."

"Senseless. She's got Maggie because she thinks Maggie knows
too much. She killed Alice immediately. It's been two hours since
anyone's seen Maggie. We've got to find them. Now!" John said.

"Watson's got a bunch of people combing the other end of the island. Toot and his buddies are searching this end. John, you and
Dickie come with me."

"If anything's happened to Maggie, I'll kill myself," Dickie said.
"She's the first person that cared enough to help us all out over here.
It's all my fault. I thought she'd tell me when we was gonna lure the
killer. I still can't believe S.J. would do that." He wiped his eyes and
followed John and Hammond to the sheriff's car.

Twenty-five

" I've kept you alive longer than I planned. You'll tell everybody what I did," S.J. Said.

"You're sick, S.J. You need help. Maybe you won't have to go to jail. You can rest. In a hospital. People will take care of you. Untie my hands. I'll help you," Maggie mumbled. "You don't have enough red ribbon with you. You can't kill me without a lot of ribbon."

Maggie felt another blow across her back, harder than the previous blows. Her breathing came in shallow snatches. Memories from the week floated through her mind. Her relationship with John never had a chance to fully develop. Rosemont. The Arden Design firm. Friends and family. She wanted to remember more of her life. Trying to tell herself to stay awake, stay alive, she fought the demons clouding her mind. Her will to live battled the blows that were steadily beating her into oblivion.

And then, a fresh, cool ocean breeze was penetrating the haze of Maggie's mind. Quick, hurried footsteps and shouting brought her back to consciousness. She heard John's voice screaming her name. Maggie tried to move. She tried to open her eyes. The bright light felt like cactus needles penetrating her entire body. Hammond was leading S.J. out the door. Her hands were cuffed behind her back.

Dickie stood above Maggie. Tears were streaming down his face. John knelt beside her and gently put his arms under her neck.

"Don't talk," he said. "Stay still. We're taking you to the mainland. The hospital staff is waiting for you. Maggie, you're alive."

Twenty-six

Maggie sat up in bed, fluffed her pillows, and tried not to scratch. The chicken pox had hit with full force while she was recovering in the hospital. The ocean view from the window of the Heywards' guest room was pleasant this morning. Maggie watched John and his sailboat heading downwind. A light breeze drifted through the windows. Maude walked in, carrying breakfast on a sterling silver platter.

"Lord, child, I'm so happy to see you still alive. To think what you went through. And Doc Matthews says you're recovering fully. All them broken ribs. And the cuts and bruises inside your mouth, on your head, and on your poor body. It's a miracle you ain't dead."

"You've said that for the last two mornings. Doctor Matthews explained that I only had a few light blows on my head. S.J. had planned to kill me with the driftwood after she tortured me."

"Eat your breakfast and don't think no more on it. You got to get well."

"Hammond's coming over this morning. We need to tie up the loose ends. There are still some questions that he can answer. After that, I never want to think about it again. How much longer am I going to itch?"

"You'll be better soon. After you eat, take the Benadryl. Another soda bath wouldn't hurt none either. Granny Jones sent some herbs over to mix with it. Help with all that soreness you got, too. Only happened a few weeks ago. You can't get better overnight."

"You and John are pampering me, not that I'm complaining, mind you. This has been the most restful part of my vacation. If I just didn't hurt from the beating and itch from the chicken pox. What's that noise on the stairs? Sounds like Dickie."

"I ain't waiting another minute," Dickie called over his shoulder to Clarence, who had been turning visitors away.

He walked into the bedroom with a red plastic bowl full of garde-nias. The smell reminded Maggie of her grandmother's perfume. To her, it was the smell of Southern hospitality and graciousness.

"Oh, Dickie, the flowers are wonderful! Does Sally Jo know you brought them?"

"She and the rest of the Red-Eye regulars are downstairs. Can they come up, too? We done been over here six times in the last week. Wanna make sure you're okay."

"Tell everybody to come up. I want to hear about the Beach Float." Before Maggie could get the entire sentence out of her mouth, Little Lavender popped through the door. His morning at-tire matched the purple lilacs blooming by the steps of the Heywards' door. Toot Sweet, Terrance, the Red-Eye Quar-tet—without their instruments—and Sally Jo, whose smile seemed wider than the ocean outside the window, packed into the guest room. They began to talk, all at the same time. They were telling the same story, but each one had a different version.

"Wow, your face looks like Sam Millet's did after that firecracker exploded. You gonna be okay?" Terrance asked.

"The chicken pox makes it worse," Maggie said. "I may have to have minor plastic surgery. We won't know for sure until all the pox are gone. My back looks much worse. But all the ribs will heal, and circulation is finally normal in my feet and legs. In no time, I'm coming to the Red-Eye to have a cold beer, in a clean glass, before I go back to Rosemont."

"You can't go home 'til after next Saturday," Dickie said.

"Why not?" Maggie asked.

"We've saved the best news 'til last. We got enough money to clean up the bar and send six kids to camp, but there's something even better. Sally Jo's ticket won the big prize. We done won the

180

two nights in the honeymoon suite at Seaward Inn. And that's just what we gonna do. Ain't it, Sally Jo?"

"We're getting married next Saturday at Liberty Oak. Reverend Pittman says he'll do it, and I'm making a list of what to do to plan it, just like you taught me. Maggie, will you be our maid of honor?"

Maggie smiled. Dickie needed Sally Jo's settling influence, and she would keep the Red-Eye in business.

"I'd be delighted. That's the best news! You have a whole year to plan the next Beach Float. Choose a good cause and promote it. I'll be back to help you celebrate your first anniversary of marriage and fundraising. Thanks to all of you for looking for me and getting the *Mary Grace* to take me to the mainland. You're a bunch of great friends. Sally Jo, you decide what you want me to wear Saturday. I'd better warn you, though, I don't look good in neon. Or pink rollers. Something softer, I think."

"Aw, shucks, Maggie, you got pretty clothes. We'll cover those poxes with makeup if we have too. Mama'll know what to do."

"Enough," Maude said. "She needs to rest now. Scat, all of you. You can see she's just fine. Now go do something constructive for a change."

Toot Sweet stepped up to the bed and said in a quiet voice, "Dickie says you're loaning me the money to get my Caddy painted. I'll take you for a ride when you can git up."

"I'm proud of you, Toot. You can pay me back with the money you earn at the oyster shucking plant. John told me Tom Murphy got you the job."

"Six dollars an hour. I ain't never seen that much money. I'll work hard. I know you and John asked Tom to do that. Thanks again. We'll see you Saturday. Git well quick."

"See you Saturday." Maggie watched her visitors file out the door and down the hall.

"Marilyn and Greg Meyers called again this morning," Maude said. "I ain't told them how bad you was. They staying out there another week. I told them you'd call tonight. Get some rest now. Sheriff Hammond'll be here after a while. You gonna need all your strength to deal with that man. He's still a-threatening to haul you and Dickie off to the big house. Says you nearly got yourself killed, interfering with his business."

Maggie rubbed the satin on Grandmother Heyward's bed jacket. Smooth and gentle cloth melted into her itching skin. From the corner of her eye, she noticed the sailboat coming about and tacking upwind. John must be heading toward his slip and home for lunch.

Maggie knew that panic was a mild word for his reaction when he'd realized she had disappeared. This was the first day he'd left the house since she'd been out of the hospital. They had spent hours discussing Alice. He had rejected what S.J. had said about Catherine's death. It had been an accident in his mind, and it would stay that way, Maggie knew.

Heavy footsteps lumbered down the hallway toward the quiet bedroom. Maggie took a deep breath. The time had finally come to deal with Sheriff Hammond.

He didn't waste any time with small talk. "You're lucky to be alive," he said, "and not in jail where you and Dickie ought to be."

"You're not the first to pronounce those words over me. Please, sit and relax, let's declare a truce. I'm sorry that I suspected you."

"Rightly so. My daddy gave me some good advice. I'm gonna pass it on to you. He learned it from a man named Will Rogers. 'It isn't what we don't know that gives us trouble; it's what we know that ain't so.' "

"My natural retort is from Thomas Huxley: 'Every great advance in natural knowledge has involved the absolute rejection of authority.' Let's quit trying to out-quote each other. Most of my investigations led me in the wrong direction, but you've got to give me credit for the poachers. You'd been trying to catch them for months."

"I concede that. I also had my badge as an advantage. I wanted to keep you from becoming involved. I didn't want no city lady killed on my island."

"I have to ask: S.J., is she...?"

"Having her psychiatric exam this morning. Drugs have probably burned her brains. Seems to think she killed you, too."

Maggie shook her head. "Bizarre. I never suspected her. She was so normal when I was around her. Robert Davis thought so, too. He's planning to stay and rebuild the Shipyard Marina. He may buy Alice and Ralph's property, join it with the Heywards' as a wildlife sanctuary.

"What made you suspect S.J.?" Maggie finally asked. She'd recalled the entire week in her mind so many times. A lot of the events made sense in light of her full knowledge.

"The sun-watch. Michael's parents asked for it to be returned. When I questioned S.J. and the art students, she had it on her arm. When I asked, she claimed it was hers. A student told me later it wasn't true. And by the way, it was one of Joe's cohorts who shot at you at the marina. He'd taken Toot's Caddy on the pretense that he'd paint it.

"The ribbon found on the beach with Alice had only S.J.'s prints on it. S.J. was getting sloppy. Pressure was too great for her. She lured Michael to the spot where she painted in the lagoon. I was closing in, but I never had real proof 'til we found you. I'm glad we did. I never understood what you thought you was doing by trying to lure the murderer from the beach party, though."

"I didn't know who would follow me, or if it would work."

"S.J. did say that when you was at her party, she thought you recognized the picture she painted at the lagoon. Said you left so quickly that she'd thought you knew. Even then, she wasn't thinking clearly. It did make her mighty suspicious of you. Well, that about does it, I guess."

"Does what?" John asked. He walked quietly into the room.

"Maggie and I were tying up loose ends. Guess Tom Murphy and I'll go fishing tomorrow. Seaward's settling into its quiet life again."

"Not for long," John said. "I just heard the news on the radio. The South Carolina legislature finally is voting on the bill for state support for a bridge to our island. By this time next year, we'll have to leave for the summer and let the 'gators entertain the tourists."

"Don't worry, John. Maybe it won't happen," Maggie said.

"It could help when we have another emergency. Quicker access to the mainland. The *Mary Grace* will always run, even as a tourist attraction."

"Sometimes change ain't all bad," Hammond said. "It'll make my job easier. More deputies on the payroll. Guess I can still go fishing. See you all Saturday at the big wedding."

Hammond waved and walked out. John sat very carefully on the bed next to Maggie and took her hand.

"I'd give you a kiss, but there's not a place on your face that's not covered with pox or cuts," he said with a laugh.

Maggie smiled and John kissed her lightly on the tips of her fingers.

Twenty-seven

The Atlantic Ocean lapped peacefully along the edge of grainy, white sand. A perfect wedding day for Dickie and Sally Jo. Sparkling and calm, the spring tide complemented the festivities surrounding Liberty Oak.

Maggie surveyed the group gathered to witness the nuptials. It was an eclectic group of well-wishers. Even Little Lavender's lilac suede suit coat added a pastel finish to the couple's choice of decoration. Smoothing the silk folds of her soft coral dress, Maggie sneaked a glance at John. He returned the look with a big grin.

Maggie's thoughts were not as calm as the morning tide. She had not reached a final decision about her career choices. She'd stepped in by phone, given the final push for the finishing touches of Jean Monroe's dining room. Her colleagues in Rosemont promised they wouldn't use any shade of red on the dining room chairs. Her relationship with John wasn't that organized. She returned his grin with her most brilliant smile. The Reverend Pittman said the amens. Whooping, laughter, and general glee could be heard rippling through the crowd.

Dickie squeezed Maggie with a huge bear hug. "Wish you wouldn't leave today," he said.

"I'm afraid I have to," she answered. "I've already promised to be back for the Liberty Float next year. Maybe I'll come sooner." She glanced at John. He and Tom Murphy were reaching for champagne at the beach shack bar. Maggie decided to join them.

"Guess you heard the news," Tom said.

"News? What news?" Maggie asked.

"The bridge bill was defeated by the legislature late last night. Close vote, but our strategy worked. Gotta get Julie and the children packed up. We're leaving on the one o'clock run of the *Mary Grace*. Stay in touch, Maggie."

He waved and walked over to gather his clan for their departure.

"Kick your sandals off. We're going for a slow walk," John said, reaching for Maggie's hand.

The noise of the wedding crowd receded as John and Maggie slowly followed the beach toward the south inlet.

"Ralph's decided not to come back to Seaward. He and the family want to sell to me. I think I'll do it. This side of the island will always be protected. Traffic lights and stop signs won't pop up, and fast food won't be served on the Heyward Wildlife Preserve."

"Maude's home cooking will still be available. In spite of the murders and chicken pox, I've enjoyed my stay and the gracious hospitality of Maude and Clarence."

"I know they want you to come back," John replied, "to buy S.J.'s pink palace. Paint it sand dune beige and run your design service from there. You're still considering that, right?"

"Yes, I'm considering. The house has enormous potential. It needs simplicity, natural wood, bleached oak, and white-washed furnishings with linen and cotton fabrics."

"That sounds like more than considering to me." John put his arm around Maggie's waist and pulled her toward him.

"Maude and Clarence will be here for hours celebrating with the newlyweds," he said. "Let's go back to my house, check on Possum, and have a quiet lunch. Spend the rest of the day with me, Maggie."

Maggie intertwined her fingers with John's as they headed back down the beach.

About the Author

Henry O. Robertson

Linda Shirley Robertson lives on an island off the coast of South Carolina with her husband, Henry. She was born in Greenville, South Carolina, and received her B.A. degree from Winthrop University. Ms. Robertson's work has been published in regional and national publications. In 1982, she co-authored South Carolina's International Greenville. In recent years, she has written a series of short stories depicting Southern life with wit and authenticity. *Murder Swings the Tide* is her first Maggie Stewart mystery.

Colophon

Tabby Manse ™

Coastal Villages Press is dedicated to helping
to preserve the timeless values of traditional
places along America's Atlantic coast—
building houses to endure through
the centuries; living in harmony
with the natural environment;
honoring history, culture,
family and friends—
and helping to
make
these
values
relevant
today.
This
book
was
completed on
September 3, 2003, at Stonington, Maine.
It was designed and set by George Graham Trask
in Adobe Garamond, a rendition of a typeface created by
Claude Garamond in Paris in 1530.